F. SCOTT FITZGERALD

THE GREAT GATSBY

Preface and notes
by Matthew J. Bruccoli

SCRIBNER
PUBLISHED BY SIMON & SCHUSTER
NEW YORK LONDON TORONTO SYDNEY SINGAPORE

SCRIBNER
1230 Avenue of the Americas
New York, NY 10020

First Scribner trade paperback edition 2003

SCRIBNER and design are trademarks
of Macmillan Library Reference USA, Inc., used under license
by Simon & Schuster, the publisher of this work.

For information about special discounts for bulk purchases,
please contact Simon & Schuster Special Sales:
1-800-456-6798 or business@simonandschuster.com

Manufactured in the United States of America

40

ISBN 0-684-80152-3

Map from the Cambridge Edition of the Works of F. Scott
Fitzgerald is reprinted by permission of Cambridge
University Press.

Foreword to the
Seventy-Fifth Anniversary Edition

♦

F. Scott Fitzgerald, *The Great Gatsby,*
and the House of Scribner

Matthew J. Bruccoli

Would the 25 cent press keep *Gatsby* in the public eye—or *is the book unpopular?* Has it *had* its chance? Would a popular reissue in that series with a preface *not* by me but by one of its admirers—I can maybe pick one—make it a favorite with class rooms, profs, lovers of English prose—anybody. But to die, so completely and unjustly after having given so much. Even now there is little published in American fiction that doesn't slightly bare [*sic*] my stamp—in a *small* way I was an original.

—Fitzgerald to Perkins, 20 May 1940

Early in November 1924 Maxwell Perkins received the typescript of a novel sent from France by F. Scott Fitzgerald. It was titled *The Great Gatsby* or perhaps

Trimalchio in West Egg. Perkins ("I think the novel is a wonder.") and Fitzgerald ("I think that at last I've done something really my own, but how good 'my own' is remains to be seen.") knew that it was an achievement, but neither one suspected that the novel would become the most widely read, translated, admired, imitated, and studied twentieth-century work of American fiction. Certainly no one connected with the publication of *The Great Gatsby* envisioned a seventy-fifth anniversary celebration of what is the tenth printing of the fourteenth Scribner edition: an estimated ten million Scribner copies sold as of the year 2000—exclusive of foreign editions.

That the House of Scribner boasted the most brilliant American fiction list during the twenties resulted from Perkin's editorial acumen, as well as from the reciprocal loyalty between authors and publishers. Most writers are insecure; Scribner authors felt safe—although, like all writers, they complained about the inadequate advertising of their books. The Perkins/Scribner commitment to Fitzgerald is documented by the record of *Gatsby,* which was a disappointing publishing venture in 1925. The first printing of 20,870 copies published on 10 April and priced at $2.00 sold out; a second printing of 3,000 copies was manufactured in August. Contrary to the myth that Fitzgerald died out-of-print, unsold copies of this second printing were in the warehouse when he died in December 1940. Fitzgerald's last royalty statement reported sales of seven copies of *Gatsby* in the first half of 1940. The Fitzgerald obituaries resulted in the sale of the remaining copies in stock. In 1942 Scribner reprinted 260 copies of *The Great Gatsby*: an unprofitable endeavor to make the novel available to the few readers who wanted it.

As a memorial, Perkins conceived the plan for a 1941 volume of Fitzgerald's unfinished novel, *The Last Tycoon,* edited by Edmund Wilson, with *The Great Gatsby* and short stories. It catalyzed the re-appraisal of Fitzgerald that led to the great revival in the fifties. The first Scribner Student's Edition was published in 1957. The rest is literary history.

Exegit monumentum aere perennius. *

Matthew J. Bruccoli

*"He completed a monument more durable than bronze."—Horace

Preface

♦

What little I've accomplished has been by the most laborious and uphill work, and I wish now I'd *never* relaxed or looked back—but said at the end of *The Great Gatsby:* "I've found my line—from now on this comes first. This is my immediate duty—without this I am nothing."

—F. Scott Fitzgerald

The Great Gatsby does not proclaim the nobility of the human spirit; it is not politically correct; it does not reveal how to solve the problems of life; it delivers no fashionable or comforting messages. It is just a masterpiece.

The best reason to read literature is for pleasure. One gauge of F. Scott Fitzgerald's achievement is that many admiring readers are unaware of the complexity of *The Great Gatsby* because the novel is a pleasure to read. It is therefore necessary to invoke his 1922 pre-*Gatsby* declaration: "I want to write something *new*—something extraordinary and beautiful and simple + intricately patterned." Masterpieces are not accidents. Geniuses know what they are doing or trying to do. They need luck, but knowing how to use the luck is an essential element of a writer's equipment.

F. Scott Fitzgerald (1896–1940) was a romantic and even tragic figure: a brilliant writer who achieved success with his first novel (*This Side of Paradise*, 1920), participated in the glamorous expatriate life in France during the Nineteen-Twenties, and then experienced a series of personal and professional blows during the Thirties. The Fitzgerald legend has attracted readers to his work; but his words matter—not the mostly distorted and inaccurate anecdotes of dissipation. Between 1920 and 1940 he published four novels, including *Tender Is the Night*; a play; 160 short stories; and essays. He was writing a superb Hollywood novel, *The Last Tycoon*, when he died. Assessing his career for his daughter Scottie he wrote from Hollywood at a low point in 1939: "I am not a great man, but sometimes I think the impersonal and objective quality of my talent, and the sacrifices of it, in pieces, to preserve its essential value has some sort of epic grandeur."

Fitzgerald was not the playboy of American literature, although certain fans like to think that he was an irresponsible writer. He was an alcoholic—as were other major American writers—but he was a serious writer and a hard worker. He did not scribble *The Great Gatsby* drunk. The novel had a three-year process of evolution, and Fitzgerald tested his material in the short stories that preceded *The Great Gatsby*. The gestation of the characters and themes can be readily observed in "Dice, Brass Knuckles & Guitar" (1923), "The 'Sensible Thing'" (1924), and particularly "Winter Dreams" (1922). "Absolution" (1924) was salvaged from a lost early version of a novel that became *The Great Gatsby.* The novel developed through layers of drafts and achieved its ultimate brilliance when Fitzgerald revised and rewrote it in the galley proofs. At the stage when most authors are finished with their work he was still perfecting *The Great Gatsby.* The published facsimiles of Fitzgerald's manuscripts and works-in-progress provide instruction on the art of his fiction, which was the art of rewriting.

The Great Gatsby is a classic—a novel that is read spontaneously by pleasure-seekers and under duress by students. A popular classroom fallacy holds that classics are universal and timeless. Literature has staying power, but it is subject to metamorphosis. Every reader's response to a work of fiction is determined by his or her presuppositional bias, beliefs, experience, and knowledge.

Fitzgerald ebulliently proclaimed in 1920 that "An author ought to write for the youth of his generation, the critics of the next, and the schoolmasters of ever afterward." Although this edict—perhaps a prophecy—was triumphantly fulfilled by *The Great Gatsby,* the novel was written by a man of his own time about his time. *The Great Gatsby* was published in 1925; therefore many of its details now seem as remote as those in the world of Charles Dickens's fiction. Great fiction is great social history; Fitzgerald's work has become automatically identified with an American decade: The Jazz Age (which he named) or The Roaring Twenties or The Boom. Since *The Great Gatsby* is the defining novel of the Twenties, which have become trivialized and vulgarized by people who weren't there, it is necessary and useful to provide a corrective assessment of that era and Fitzgerald's response to it. The Twenties were not a ten-year binge during which everybody got rich and danced the Charleston in speakeasies while drinking bootleg hooch. Certainly the reaction to America's participation in World War I—which ended on 11 November 1918—triggered disillusionment, moral reevaluation, social experiment, and hedonism. Although Fitzgerald joined the parties and chronicled them, he wrote in judgment. The Twenties were primarily an era of possibilities and aspiration—a dominant Fitzgerald theme. In "Echoes of the Jazz Age" he wrote: "It was an age of miracles, it was an age of art, it was an age of excess, and it was an age of satire." It was also an age of achievement, especially in American literature: Ernest Hemingway, William Faulkner, Thomas Wolfe, Willa Cather, Sinclair Lewis, Ring Lardner, Eugene O'Neill, John Dos Passos, Wallace Stevens, e. e. cummings, Ezra Pound, T. S. Eliot.

The novel is appropriately set in the get-rich-quick decade that brought about the organization of crime as a concomitant of Prohibition. Gatsby's criminal activities are kept mysterious, but it is evident that he has been a bootlegger. The Twenties were a time of stock-market speculation and peculation—though penny-ante stuff compared to the Eighties—and Gatsby is involved with stolen securities. On 3 September 1929 the Dow-Jones Industrial Average reached a high of 381; it fell to 261 on 28 October. (It reached a low of 41 in 1932; in 1995 it broke 5,000.) The Wall Street crash marked the end of the Twenties boom and initiated the Great Depression of the Thirties. What Fitzgerald called "the most expensive orgy in history" was over.

An essential aspect of the American-ness and the historicity of *The Great Gatsby* is that it is about money. The

Land of Opportunity promised the chance for financial success. Gatsby, who makes his fortune in ways never envisioned by Benjamin Franklin, does not understand how money works in society. He innocently expects that he can buy anything—especially Daisy. She is for sale, but he doesn't have the right currency.

It has become convenient to refer to *The Great Gatsby* as "the great American novel." If this phrase means anything, it means that the novel is the great work of fiction with defining American thematic qualities and that James Gatz/ Jay Gatsby is the great American character. (Adherents of Huck Finn take issue and umbrage.) Gatsby is the American self-made—indeed, self-invented—man. He believes in the American Dream of success ("the orgastic future"); he fulfills it; he confuses it with Daisy; he is betrayed by it. The appellation *great* as applied to Gatsby reverberates with irony. He is truly great by virtue of his capacity to commit himself to his aspirations. Yet at the same time the adjective indicates the tawdry and exaggerated aspects of his life: Hurry, hurry, hurry! Step right up and see the Great Gatsby! (Tom Buchanan describes Gatsby's car as a "circus wagon.") It is crucial to differentiate the ostentatious Gatsby from the admirable Gatsby. Thus Nick instructs the reader in the fourth paragraph of the novel:

> If personality is an unbroken series of successful gestures, then there was something gorgeous about him, some heightened sensitivity to the promises of life, as if he were related to one of those intricate machines that register earthquakes ten thousand miles away. This responsiveness had nothing to do with that flabby impressionability which is dignified under the name

of the "creative temperament"—it was an extraordinary gift for hope, a romantic readiness such as I have never found in any other person and which it is not likely I shall ever find again.

Great fiction creates memorable characters; and the essentially incredible Jay Gatsby is made convincing by means of narrative point of view and narrative structure. Gatsby is the hero, but Nick Carraway is the central figure. Most of Gatsby's speech is retold by Nick, who is the voice of the novel and the voice of the novelist. The structural plan depends on Nick, the *partially involved narrator* who documents all the events and relates them in the order he learned them—except for the details of Gatsby's biography at the opening of Chapter VI. Nick serves as a trustworthy reporter and, reluctantly, as judge: "No—Gatsby turned out all right at the end; it is what preyed on Gatsby, what foul dust floated in the wake of his dreams that temporarily closed out my interest in the abortive sorrows and short-winded elations of men."

Complexity for the sake of complexity is bad writing; the structure of *The Great Gatsby* is functional. The reader is required to reconstruct the actual chronology of events, much of which is revealed in flashbacks—thereby becoming a collaborator in the narrative. Most important, the reader is responsible for sorting and re-ordering the lies and truths about Gatsby. Thus:

Chapter III: Nick hears rumors at the party about the mysterious Gatsby.

Chapter IV: Gatsby tells Nick a mostly false autobiography during their car ride to New York; Jordan Baker tells

Nick about Gatsby's courtship of Daisy in 1917.

Chapter VI: Nick relates biography of Gatsby's youth: "He told me all this very much later, but I've put it down here with the idea of exploding those first wild rumors about his antecedents, which weren't even faintly true"; Nick retells Gatsby's account of falling in love with Daisy—but impressionistically, not in Gatsby's words.

Chapter VII: Gatsby proves that he went to Oxford; Tom Buchanan reveals Gatsby's bootlegging activities.

Chapter VIII: "It was this night that he told me the strange story of his youth with Dan Cody . . ." (see Chapter VI); Nick repeats Gatsby's account of his falling in love with Daisy and the consummation, his war record, Daisy's unfaithfulness (without source), and his return to Louisville after the war.

Chapter IX: Meyer Wolfshiem tells Nick about his partnership with Gatsby; Mr. Gatz shows Gatsby's boyhood schedule to Nick.

However, there are integral chronological problems in *The Great Gatsby*. The present-time events occupy three months in 1922, from Nick's dinner with the Buchanans in early June to Gatsby's funeral in early September, followed by Nick's departure in October. Elapsed time is unaccounted for during June and July; too much action is crowded into late August. There are inconsistent time signals. These difficulties partly result from Fitzgerald's general language ("a few days," "several weeks," "about six weeks"); but the chronology for June and July events was blurred by his decision to transpose Chapters II and III between manuscript and typescript. Here is the time-scheme for the summer 1922 action:

page 16. lines 10–11 "In two weeks it'll be the longest day in the year." About 7 June: Nick visits Buchanans.

30.22 "a few days before the Fourth of July": Nick, Tom, and Myrtle go to New York.

62.14–15 "in midsummer": Nick begins dating Jordan—some time in July.

69.1 "past month": Nick has known Gatsby for a month by the time they drive to New York in late July; therefore Nick had attended first Gatsby party in late June.

82.27 "about six weeks" since Buchanan dinner (c. 7 June); therefore late July when Jordan tells Nick about Daisy and Gatsby. Reunion of Daisy and Gatsby is a few days later.

107.20 "several weeks" between reunion and the Sunday when Tom and friends come to Gatsby's house; therefore mid-August.

110.17 "the following Saturday": Tom and Daisy attend Gatsby's party—mid- or late August.

120.1 "a week ago": Gatsby replaces servants and parties stop—late August.

120.26 "almost the last" day of summer, c. Labor Day. Plaza Hotel confrontation and death of Myrtle.

175.4 "the third day" after Gatsby's murder: Mr. Gatz arrives on "a warm September day."

It is appropriate and utilitarian that *The Great Gatsby* have an "intricately patterned" chronology, for time is a major theme in the novel—and in all of Fitzgerald's best fiction. The novel begins "In my younger and more vulnerable years . . ." and ends "borne back ceaselessly into the past." It uses some 450 time-words, including 87 appearances of *time*. Episodes are reinforced by time symbolism: the Buchanan lawn is described as "jumping over sundials"; Nick's famous list of people who attended Gatsby's parties is written on a timetable; Gatsby knocks over a clock during his reunion with Daisy; and Klipspringer plays "In the meantime, In between time——".

The time theme encompasses the related themes of mutability and loss. Fitzgerald wrote in 1924 while he was working on *Gatsby:* "That's the whole burden of this novel—the loss of those illusions that give such color to the world so that you don't care whether things are true or false as long as they partake of the magical glory." Gatsby does not accept the process of time. His most memorable statement is: " 'Can't repeat the past?' he cried incredulously. 'Why of course you can!' " Ultimately the novel is about American history, compounding the time theme and the aspiration theme. *The Great Gatsby* closes with Nick's eloquent broodings on the unfulfilled potentialities of the new world—"for a transitory enchanted moment man must have held his breath in the presence of this continent . . . face to face for the last time in history with something commensurate to his capacity for wonder."

F. Scott Fitzgerald died in 1940 fearing that he was a failure, forgotten. *The Great Gatsby* led the Fitzgerald rediscovery and restoration of 1945–50 because it is a miracle—though not his only miracle. Literary miracles are the work of writers who come closer than other writers to expressing what is in their minds through innate genius augmented by control, technique, craft.

Matthew J. Bruccoli
The University of South Carolina, 1992

The Great Gatsby

Then wear the gold hat, if that will move her;
  If you can bounce high, bounce for her too,
Till she cry "Lover, gold-hatted, high-bouncing lover,
  I must have you!"

—THOMAS PARKE D'INVILLIERS

ONCE AGAIN
TO
ZELDA

CHAPTER I

♦

In my younger and more vulnerable years my father gave me some advice that I've been turning over in my mind ever since.

"Whenever you feel like criticizing anyone," he told me, "just remember that all the people in this world haven't had the advantages that you've had."

He didn't say any more but we've always been unusually communicative in a reserved way and I understood that he meant a great deal more than that. In consequence I'm inclined to reserve all judgements, a habit that has opened up many curious natures to me and also made me the victim of not a few veteran bores. The abnormal mind is quick to detect and attach itself to this quality when it appears in a normal person, and so it came about that in college I was unjustly accused of being a politician, because I was privy to the secret griefs of wild, unknown men. Most of the confidences were unsought—frequently I have feigned sleep, preoccupation or a hostile levity when I realized by some unmistakable sign that an intimate revelation was quivering on the horizon—for the intimate revelations of young men or at least the terms in which they express them are usually plagiaristic and marred by obvious suppressions. Reserving judgements is a matter of infinite hope. I am still a little afraid of missing something if I forget that, as my father snobbishly suggested and I snobbishly repeat, a sense of the fundamental decencies is parcelled out unequally at birth.

And, after boasting this way of my tolerance, I come to the admission that it has a limit. Conduct may be founded on the hard rock or the wet marshes but after a certain point I don't care what it's founded on. When I came back from the East last autumn I felt that I wanted the world to be in uniform and at a sort of moral attention forever; I wanted no more riotous excursions with privileged glimpses into the human heart. Only Gatsby, the man who gives his name to this book, was exempt from my reaction—Gatsby who represented everything for which I have an unaffected scorn. If personality is an unbroken series of successful gestures, then there was something gorgeous about him, some heightened sensitivity to the promises of life, as if he were related to one of those intricate machines that register earthquakes ten thousand miles away. This responsiveness had nothing to do with that flabby impressionability which is dignified under the name of the "creative temperament"—it was an extraordinary gift for hope, a romantic readiness such as I have never found in any other person and which it is not likely I shall ever find again. No—Gatsby turned out all right at the end; it is what preyed on Gatsby, what foul dust floated in the wake of his dreams that temporarily closed out my interest in the abortive sorrows and short-winded elations of men.

My family have been prominent, well-to-do people in this middle-western city for three generations. The Carraways are something of a clan and we have a tradition that we're descended from the Dukes of Buccleuch, but the actual founder of my line was my grandfather's brother who came here in fifty-one, sent a substitute to the Civil War and started the wholesale hardware business that my father carries on today.

I never saw this great-uncle but I'm supposed to look like him—with special reference to the rather hard-boiled painting that hangs in Father's office. I graduated from New Haven in 1915, just a quarter of a century after my father, and a little later I participated in that delayed Teutonic migration known as the Great War. I enjoyed the counter-raid so thoroughly that I came back restless. Instead of being the warm center of the world the middle-west now seemed like the ragged edge of the universe—so I decided to go east and learn the bond business. Everybody I knew was in the bond business so I supposed it could support one more single man. All my aunts and uncles talked it over as if they were choosing a prep-school for me and finally said "Why—ye-es" with very grave, hesitant faces. Father agreed to finance me for a year and after various delays I came east, permanently, I thought, in the spring of twenty-two.

The practical thing was to find rooms in the city but it was a warm season and I had just left a country of wide lawns and friendly trees, so when a young man at the office suggested that we take a house together in a commuting town it sounded like a great idea. He found the house, a weather beaten cardboard bungalow at eighty a month, but at the last minute the firm ordered him to Washington and I went out to the country alone. I had a dog, at least I had him for a few days until he ran away, and an old Dodge and a Finnish woman who made my bed and cooked breakfast and muttered Finnish wisdom to herself over the electric stove.

It was lonely for a day or so until one morning some man, more recently arrived than I, stopped me on the road.

"How do you get to West Egg Village?" he asked helplessly.

I told him. And as I walked on I was lonely no longer. I was a guide, a pathfinder, an original settler. He had casually conferred on me the freedom of the neighborhood.

And so with the sunshine and the great bursts of leaves growing on the trees—just as things grow in fast movies—I had that familiar conviction that life was beginning over again with the summer.

There was so much to read for one thing and so much fine health to be pulled down out of the young breath-giving air. I bought a dozen volumes on banking and credit and investment securities and they stood on my shelf in red and gold like new money from the mint, promising to unfold the shining secrets that only Midas and Morgan and Mæcenas knew. And I had the high intention of reading many other books besides. I was rather literary in college—one year I wrote a series of very solemn and obvious editorials for the "Yale News"—and now I was going to bring back all such things into my life and become again that most limited of all specialists, the "well-rounded" man. This isn't just an epigram—life is much more successfully looked at from a single window, after all.

It was a matter of chance that I should have rented a house in one of the strangest communities in North America. It was on that slender riotous island which extends itself due east of New York and where there are, among other natural curiosities, two unusual formations of land. Twenty miles from the city a pair of enormous eggs, identical in contour and separated only by a courtesy bay, jut out into the most domesticated body of salt water in the Western Hemisphere, the great wet barnyard of Long Island Sound. They are not perfect ovals—like the egg in the Columbus story they are both crushed flat at the contact end—but their physical resemblance must be a source of perpetual confusion to the gulls that fly overhead. To the wingless a more arresting phenomenon is their dissimilarity in every particular except shape and size.

I lived at West Egg, the—well, the less fashionable of the two, though this is a most superficial tag to express the bizarre and not a little sinister contrast between them. My house was at the very tip of the egg, only fifty yards from the Sound, and squeezed between two huge places that rented for twelve or fifteen thousand a season. The one on my right was a colossal affair by any standard—it was a factual imitation of some Hôtel de Ville in Normandy, with a tower on one side, spanking new under a thin beard of raw ivy, and a marble swimming pool and more than forty acres of lawn and garden. It was Gatsby's mansion. Or rather, as I didn't know Mr. Gatsby it was a mansion inhabited by a gentleman of that name. My own house was an eye-sore, but it was a small eye-sore and it had been overlooked, so I had a view of the water, a partial view of my neighbor's lawn and the consoling proximity of millionaires—all for eighty dollars a month.

Across the courtesy bay the white palaces of fashionable East Egg glittered along the water and the history of the summer really begins on the evening I drove over there to have dinner with the Tom Buchanans. Daisy was my second cousin once removed and I'd known Tom in college. And just after the war I spent two days with them in Chicago.

Her husband, among various physical accomplishments, had been one of the most powerful ends that ever played football at New Haven—a national figure in a way, one of those men who reach such an acute limited excellence at twenty-one that everything afterwards savours of anti-climax. His family were enormously wealthy—even in college his freedom with money was a matter for reproach—but now he'd left Chicago and come east in a fashion that rather took your breath away: for instance he'd brought down a string of polo ponies from Lake Forest. It was hard to realize that a man in my own generation was wealthy enough to do that.

Why they came east I don't know. They had spent a year in France, for no particular reason, and then drifted here and there unrestfully wherever people played polo and were rich together. This was a permanent move, said Daisy over the telephone, but I didn't believe it—I had no sight into Daisy's heart but I felt that Tom would drift on forever seeking a little wistfully for the dramatic turbulence of some irrecoverable football game.

And so it happened that on a warm windy evening I drove

over to East Egg to see two old friends whom I scarcely knew at all. Their house was even more elaborate than I expected, a cheerful red and white Georgian Colonial mansion overlooking the bay. The lawn started at the beach and ran toward the front door for a quarter of a mile, jumping over sun-dials and brick walks and burning gardens—finally when it reached the house drifting up the side in bright vines as though from the momentum of its run. The front was broken by a line of French windows, glowing now with reflected gold, and wide open to the warm windy afternoon, and Tom Buchanan in riding clothes was standing with his legs apart on the front porch.

He had changed since his New Haven years. Now he was a sturdy, straw haired man of thirty with a rather hard mouth and a supercilious manner. Two shining, arrogant eyes had established dominance over his face and gave him the appearance of always leaning aggressively forward. Not even the effeminate swank of his riding clothes could hide the enormous power of that body—he seemed to fill those glistening boots until he strained the top lacing and you could see a great pack of muscle shifting when his shoulder moved under his thin coat. It was a body capable of enormous leverage—a cruel body.

His speaking voice, a gruff husky tenor, added to the impression of fractiousness he conveyed. There was a touch of paternal contempt in it, even toward people he liked—and there were men at New Haven who had hated his guts.

"Now, don't think my opinion on these matters is final," he seemed to say, "just because I'm stronger and more of a man than you are." We were in the same Senior Society and while we were never intimate I always had the impression that he approved of me and wanted me to like him with some harsh, defiant wistfulness of his own.

We talked for a few minutes on the sunny porch.

"I've got a nice place here," he said, his eyes flashing about restlessly.

Turning me around by one arm he moved a broad flat hand along the front vista, including in its sweep a sunken Italian garden, a half acre of deep pungent roses and a snub-nosed motor boat that bumped the tide off shore.

"It belonged to Demaine the oil man." He turned me around again, politely and abruptly. "We'll go inside."

We walked through a high hallway into a bright rosy-colored space, fragilely bound into the house by French windows at either end. The windows were ajar and gleaming white against the fresh grass outside that seemed to grow a little way into the house. A breeze blew through the room, blew curtains in at one end and out the other like pale flags, twisting them up toward the frosted wedding cake of the ceiling—and then rippled over the wine-colored rug, making a shadow on it as wind does on the sea.

The only completely stationary object in the room was an enormous couch on which two young women were buoyed up as though upon an anchored balloon. They were both in white and their dresses were rippling and fluttering as if they had just been blown back in after a short flight around the house. I must have stood for a few moments listening to the whip and snap of the curtains and the groan of a picture on the wall. Then there was a boom as Tom Buchanan shut the rear windows and the caught wind died out about the room and the curtains and the rugs and the two young women ballooned slowly to the floor.

The younger of the two was a stranger to me. She was extended full length at her end of the divan, completely motionless and with her chin raised a little as if she were balancing something on it which was quite likely to fall. If she saw me out of the corner of her eyes she gave no hint of it—indeed I was almost surprised into murmuring an apology for having disturbed her by coming in.

The other girl, Daisy, made an attempt to rise—she leaned slightly forward with a conscientious expression—then she laughed, an absurd, charming little laugh, and I laughed too and came forward into the room.

"I'm p-paralyzed with happiness."

She laughed again, as if she said something very witty, and held my hand for a moment, looking up into my face, promising that there was no one in the world she so much wanted to see. That was a way she had. She hinted in a murmur that the surname of the balancing girl was Baker. (I've heard it said that Daisy's murmur was only to make people lean toward her; an irrelevant criticism that made it no less charming.)

At any rate Miss Baker's lips fluttered, she nodded at me almost imperceptibly and then quickly tipped her head back again—the object she was balancing had obviously tottered a little and given her something of a fright. Again a sort of apology arose to my lips. Almost any exhibition of complete self sufficiency draws a stunned tribute from me.

I looked back at my cousin who began to ask me questions in her low, thrilling voice. It was the kind of voice that the ear follows up and down as if each speech is an arrangement of notes that will never be played again. Her face was sad and lovely with bright things in it, bright eyes and a bright passionate mouth—but there was an excitement in her voice that men who had cared for her found difficult to forget: a singing compulsion, a whispered "Listen," a promise that she had done gay, exciting things just a while since and that there were gay, exciting things hovering in the next hour.

I told her how I had stopped off in Chicago for a day on my way east and how a dozen people had sent their love through me.

"Do they miss me?" she cried ecstatically.

"The whole town is desolate. All the cars have the left rear wheel painted black as a mourning wreath and there's a persistent wail all night along the North Shore."

"How gorgeous! Let's go back, Tom. Tomorrow!" Then she added irrelevantly, "You ought to see the baby."

"I'd like to."

"She's asleep. She's two years old. Haven't you ever seen her?"

"Never."

"Well, you ought to see her. She's——"

Tom Buchanan who had been hovering restlessly about the room stopped and rested his hand on my shoulder.

"What you doing, Nick?"

"I'm a bond man."

"Who with?"

I told him.

"Never heard of them," he remarked decisively.

This annoyed me.

"You will," I answered shortly. "You will if you stay in the East."

"Oh, I'll stay in the East, don't you worry," he said,

glancing at Daisy and then back at me as if he were alert for something more. "I'd be a God Damn fool to live anywhere else."

At this point Miss Baker said "Absolutely!" with such suddenness that I started—it was the first word she had uttered since I came into the room. Evidently it surprised her as much as it did me, for she yawned and with a series of rapid, deft movements stood up into the room.

"I'm stiff," she complained. "I've been lying on that sofa for as long as I can remember."

"Don't look at me," Daisy retorted. "I've been trying to get you to New York all afternoon."

"No thanks," said Miss Baker to the four cocktails just in from the pantry, "I'm absolutely in training."

Her host looked at her incredulously.

"You are!" He took down his drink as if it were a drop in the bottom of a glass. "How you ever get anything done is beyond me."

I looked at Miss Baker wondering what it was she "got done." I enjoyed looking at her. She was a slender, small-breasted girl with an erect carriage which she accentuated by throwing her body backward at the shoulders like a young cadet. Her grey sun-strained eyes looked back at me with polite reciprocal curiosity out of a wan, charming discontented face. It occurred to me now that I had seen her, or a picture of her, somewhere before.

"You live in West Egg," she remarked contemptuously. "I know somebody there."

"I don't know a single——"

"You must know Gatsby."

"Gatsby?" demanded Daisy. "What Gatsby?"

Before I could reply that he was my neighbor dinner was announced; wedging his tense arm imperatively under mine Tom Buchanan compelled me from the room as though he were moving a checker to another square.

Slenderly, languidly, their hands set lightly on their hips the two young women preceded us out onto a rosy-colored porch open toward the sunset where four candles flickered on the table in the diminished wind.

"Why *candles?*" objected Daisy frowning. She snapped them out with her fingers. "In two weeks it'll be the longest day in the year." She looked at us all radiantly. "Do you always watch for the longest day of the year and then miss it? I always watch for the longest day in the year and then miss it."

"We ought to plan something," yawned Miss Baker, sitting down at the table as if she were getting into bed.

"All right," said Daisy. "What'll we plan?" She turned to me helplessly. "What do people plan?"

Before I could answer her eyes fastened with an awed expression on her little finger.

"Look!" she complained. "I hurt it."

We all looked—the knuckle was black and blue.

"You did it, Tom," she said accusingly. "I know you didn't mean to but you *did* do it. That's what I get for marrying a brute of a man, a great big hulking physical specimen of a——"

"I hate that word hulking," objected Tom crossly, "even in kidding."

"Hulking," insisted Daisy.

Sometimes she and Miss Baker talked at once, unobtrusively and with a bantering inconsequence that was never quite chatter, that was as cool as their white dresses and their impersonal eyes in the absence of all desire. They were here—and they accepted Tom and me, making only a polite pleasant effort to entertain or to be entertained. They knew that presently dinner would be over and a little later the evening too would be over and casually put away. It was sharply different from the West where an evening was hurried from phase to phase toward its close in a continually disappointed anticipation or else in sheer nervous dread of the moment itself.

"You make me feel uncivilized, Daisy," I confessed on my second glass of corky but rather impressive claret. "Can't you talk about crops or something?"

I meant nothing in particular by this remark but it was taken up in an unexpected way.

"Civilization's going to pieces," broke out Tom violently. "I've gotten to be a terrible pessimist about things. Have you read 'The Rise of the Coloured Empires' by this man Goddard?"

"Why, no," I answered, rather surprised by his tone.

"Well, it's a fine book and everybody ought to read it. The idea is if we don't look out the white race will be—will be utterly submerged. It's all scientific stuff; it's been proved."

"Tom's getting very profound," said Daisy with an expression of unthoughtful sadness. "He reads deep books with long words in them. What was that word we——"

"Well, these books are all scientific," insisted Tom, glancing at her impatiently. "This fellow has worked out the whole thing. It's up to us who are the dominant race to watch out or these other races will have control of things."

"We've got to beat them down," whispered Daisy, winking ferociously toward the fervent sun.

"You ought to live in California——" began Miss Baker but Tom interrupted her by shifting heavily in his chair.

"This idea is that we're Nordics. I am and you are and you are and——" After an infinitesimal hesitation he included Daisy with a slight nod and she winked at me again, "——and we've produced all the things that go to make civilization—oh, science and art and all that. Do you see?"

There was something pathetic in his concentration as if his complacency, more acute than of old, was not enough to him any more. When, almost immediately, the telephone rang inside and the butler left the porch Daisy seized upon the momentary interruption and leaned toward me.

"I'll tell you a family secret," she whispered enthusiastically. "It's about the butler's nose. Do you want to hear about the butler's nose?"

"That's why I came over tonight."

"Well, he wasn't always a butler; he used to be the silver polisher for some people in New York that had a silver service for two hundred people. He had to polish it from morning till night until finally it began to affect his nose——"

"Things went from bad to worse," suggested Miss Baker.

"Yes. Things went from bad to worse until finally he had to give up his position."

For a moment the last sunshine fell with romantic affection upon her glowing face; her voice compelled me forward breathlessly as I listened—then the glow faded, each light deserting her with lingering regret like children leaving a pleasant street at dusk.

The butler came back and murmured something close to Tom's ear whereupon Tom frowned, pushed back his chair and without a word went inside. As if his absence quickened something within her Daisy leaned forward again, her voice glowing and singing.

"I love to see you at my table, Nick. You remind me of a—of a rose, an absolute rose. Doesn't he?" She turned to Miss Baker for confirmation. "An absolute rose?"

This was untrue. I am not even faintly like a rose. She was only extemporizing but a stirring warmth flowed from her as if her heart was trying to come out to you concealed in one of those breathless, thrilling words. Then suddenly she threw her napkin on the table and excused herself and went into the house.

Miss Baker and I exchanged a short glance consciously devoid of meaning. I was about to speak when she sat up alertly and said "Sh!" in a warning voice. A subdued impassioned murmur was audible in the room beyond and Miss Baker leaned forward, unashamed, trying to hear. The murmur trembled on the verge of coherence, sank down, mounted excitedly and then ceased altogether.

"This Mr. Gatsby you spoke of is my neighbor—" I said.

"Don't talk. I want to hear what happens."

"Is something happening?" I inquired innocently.

"You mean to say you don't know?" said Miss Baker, honestly surprised. "I thought everybody knew."

"I don't."

"Why—" she said hesitantly, "Tom's got some woman in New York."

"Got some woman?" I repeated blankly.

Miss Baker nodded.

"She might have the decency not to telephone him at dinner-time. Don't you think?"

Almost before I had grasped her meaning there was the flutter of a dress and the crunch of leather boots and Tom and Daisy were back at the table.

"It couldn't be helped!" cried Daisy with tense gayety.

She sat down, glanced searchingly at Miss Baker and then at me and continued, "I looked outdoors for a minute and it's very romantic outdoors. There's a bird on the lawn that I think must be a nightingale come over on the Cunard or White Star Line. He's singing away—" her voice sang "—It's romantic, isn't it, Tom?"

"Very romantic," he said, and then miserably to me: "If it's light enough after dinner I want to take you down to the stables."

The telephone rang inside, startlingly, and as Daisy shook her head decisively at Tom the subject of the stables, in fact all subjects, vanished into air. Among the broken fragments of the last five minutes at table I remember the candles being lit again, pointlessly, and I was conscious of wanting to look squarely at everyone and yet to avoid all eyes. I couldn't guess what Daisy and Tom were thinking but I doubt if even Miss Baker who seemed to have mastered a certain hardy skepticism was able utterly to put this fifth guest's shrill metallic urgency out of mind. To a certain temperament the situation might have seemed intriguing—my own instinct was to telephone immediately for the police.

The horses, needless to say, were not mentioned again. Tom and Miss Baker with several feet of twilight between them strolled back into the library, as if to a vigil beside a perfectly tangible body, while trying to look pleasantly interested and a little deaf I followed Daisy around a chain of connecting verandas to the porch in front. In its deep gloom we sat down side by side on a wicker settee.

Daisy took her face in her hands, as if feeling its lovely shape, and her eyes moved gradually out into the velvet dusk. I saw that turbulent emotions possessed her, so I asked what I thought would be some sedative questions about her little girl.

"We don't know each other very well, Nick," she said suddenly. "Even if we are cousins. You didn't come to my wedding."

"I wasn't back from the war."

"That's true." She hesitated. "Well, I've had a very bad time, Nick, and I'm pretty cynical about everything."

Evidently she had reason to be. I waited but she didn't say any more, and after a moment I returned rather feebly to the subject of her daughter.

"I suppose she talks, and—eats, and everything."

"Oh, yes." She looked at me absently. "Listen, Nick; let me tell you what I said when she was born. Would you like to hear?"

"Very much."

"It'll show you how I've gotten to feel about—things. Well, she was less than an hour old and Tom was God knows where. I woke up out of the ether with an utterly abandoned feeling and asked the nurse right away if it was a boy or a girl. She told me it was a girl, and so I turned my head away and wept. 'All right,' I said, 'I'm glad it's a girl. And I hope she'll be a fool—that's the best thing a girl can be in this world, a beautiful little fool.'

"You see I think everything's terrible anyhow," she went

on in a convinced way. "Everybody thinks so—the most advanced people. And I *know*. I've been everywhere and seen everything and done everything." Her eyes flashed around her in a defiant way, rather like Tom's, and she laughed with thrilling scorn. "Sophisticated—God, I'm so-phisticated!"

The instant her voice broke off, ceasing to compel my attention, my belief, I felt the basic insincerity of what she had said. It made me uneasy, as though the whole evening had been a trick of some sort to exact a contributary emotion from me. I waited, and sure enough, in a moment she looked at me with an absolute smirk on her lovely face as if she had asserted her membership in a rather distinguished secret society to which she and Tom belonged.

Inside, the crimson room bloomed with light. Tom and Miss Baker sat at either end of the long couch and she read aloud to him from the "Saturday Evening Post"—the words, murmurous and uninflected, running together in a soothing tune. The lamp-light, bright on his boots and dull on the autumn-leaf yellow of her hair, glinted along the paper as she turned a page with a flutter of slender muscles in her arms.

When we came in she held us silent for a moment with a lifted hand.

"To be continued," she said, tossing the magazine on the table, "in our very next issue."

Her body asserted itself with a restless movement of her knee, and she stood up.

"Ten o'clock," she remarked, apparently finding the time on the ceiling. "Time for this good girl to go to bed."

"Jordan's going to play in the tournament tomorrow," explained Daisy, "over at Westchester."

"Oh,—you're *Jor*dan Baker."

I knew now why her face was familiar—its pleasing contemptuous expression had looked out at me from many rotogravure pictures of the sporting life at Asheville and Hot Springs and Palm Beach. I had heard some story of her too, a critical, unpleasant story, but what it was I had forgotten long ago.

"Good night," she said softly. "Wake me at eight, won't you."

"If you'll get up."

"I will. Good night, Mr. Carraway. See you anon."

"Of course you will," confirmed Daisy. "In fact I think I'll arrange a marriage. Come over often, Nick, and I'll sort of—oh—fling you together. You know—lock you up accidentally in linen closets and push you out to sea in a boat, and all that sort of thing——"

"Good night," called Miss Baker from the stairs. "I haven't heard a word."

"She's a nice girl," said Tom after a moment. "They oughtn't to let her run around the country this way."

"Who oughtn't to?" inquired Daisy coldly.

"Her family."

"Her family is one aunt about a thousand years old. Besides, Nick's going to look after her, aren't you, Nick? She's going to spend lots of week-ends out here this summer. I think the home influence will be very good for her."

Daisy and Tom looked at each other for a moment in silence.

"Is she from New York?" I asked quickly.

"From Louisville. Our white girlhood was passed together there. Our beautiful white——"

"Did you give Nick a little heart-to-heart talk on the
veranda?" demanded Tom suddenly.

"Did I?" She looked at me. "I can't seem to remember,
but I think we talked about the Nordic race. Yes, I'm sure
we did. It sort of crept up on us and first thing you
know——"

"Don't believe everything you hear, Nick," he advised
me.

I said lightly that I had heard nothing at all, and a few
minutes later I got up to go home. They came to the door
with me and stood side by side in a cheerful square of light.
As I started my motor Daisy peremptorily called "Wait!

"I forgot to ask you something, and it's important. We
heard you were engaged to a girl out West."

"That's right," corroborated Tom kindly. "We heard
that you were engaged."

"It's a libel. I'm too poor."

"But we heard it," insisted Daisy, surprising me by opening up again in a flower-like way. "We heard it from three
people so it must be true."

Of course I knew what they were referring to, but I
wasn't even vaguely engaged. The fact that gossip had published the banns was one of the reasons I had come east.
You can't stop going with an old friend on account of
rumors and on the other hand I had no intention of being
rumored into marriage.

Their interest rather touched me and made them less
remotely rich—nevertheless, I was confused and a little dis-

gusted as I drove away. It seemed to me that the thing for Daisy to do was to rush out of the house, child in arms—but apparently there were no such intentions in her head. As for Tom the fact that he "had some woman in New York" was really less surprising than that he had been depressed by a book. Something was making him nibble at the edge of stale ideas as if his sturdy physical egotism no longer nourished his peremptory heart.

Already it was deep summer on roadhouse roofs and in front of wayside garages where new red gas-pumps sat out in pools of light, and when I reached my estate at West Egg I ran the car under its shed and sat for a while on an abandoned grass roller in the yard. The wind had blown off, leaving a loud bright night with wings beating in the trees and a persistent organ sound as the full bellows of the earth blew the frogs full of life. The silhouette of a moving cat wavered across the moonlight and turning my head to watch it I saw that I was not alone—fifty feet away a figure had emerged from the shadow of my neighbor's mansion and was standing with his hands in his pockets regarding the silver pepper of the stars. Something in his leisurely movements and the secure position of his feet upon the lawn suggested that it was Mr. Gatsby himself, come out to determine what share was his of our local heavens.

I decided to call to him. Miss Baker had mentioned him at dinner, and that would do for an introduction. But I didn't call to him for he gave a sudden intimation that he was content to be alone—he stretched out his arms toward the dark water in a curious way, and far as I was from him I could have sworn he was trembling. Involuntarily I glanced seaward—and distinguished nothing except a single green light, minute and far away, that might have been the end of a dock. When I looked once more for Gatsby he had vanished, and I was alone again in the unquiet darkness.

CHAPTER II

♦

About half way between West Egg and New York the motor-road hastily joins the railroad and runs beside it for a quarter of a mile so as to shrink away from a certain desolate area of land. This is a valley of ashes—a fantastic farm where ashes grow like wheat into ridges and hills and grotesque gardens, where ashes take the forms of houses and chimneys and rising smoke and finally, with a transcendent effort, of men who move dimly and already crumbling through the powdery air. Occasionally a line of grey cars crawls along an invisible track, gives out a ghastly creak and comes to rest, and immediately the ash-grey men swarm up with leaden spades and stir up an impenetrable cloud which screens their obscure operations from your sight.

But above the grey land and the spasms of bleak dust which drift endlessly over it, you perceive, after a moment, the eyes of Doctor T. J. Eckleburg. The eyes of Doctor T. J. Eckleburg are blue and gigantic—their retinas are one yard high. They look out of no face but, instead, from a pair of enormous yellow spectacles which pass over a nonexistent nose. Evidently some wild wag of an oculist set them there to fatten his practice in the borough of Queens and then sank down himself into eternal blindness or forgot them and moved away. But his eyes, dimmed a little by many paintless days under sun and rain, brood on over the solemn dumping ground.

The valley of ashes is bounded on one side by a small foul river, and when the drawbridge is up to let barges through, the passengers on waiting trains can stare at the dismal scene for as long as half an hour. There is always a halt there of at least a minute and it was because of this that I first met Tom Buchanan's mistress.

The fact that he had one was insisted upon wherever he was known. His acquaintances resented the fact that he turned up in popular restaurants with her and, leaving her at a table, sauntered about chatting with whomsoever he knew. Though I was curious to see her I had no desire to meet her—but I did. I went up to New York with Tom on the train one afternoon and when we stopped by the ash-heaps he jumped to his feet and taking hold of my elbow literally forced me from the car.

"We're getting off!" he insisted. "I want you to meet my girl."

I think he'd tanked up a good deal at luncheon and his determination to have my company bordered on violence. The supercilious assumption was that on Sunday afternoon I had nothing better to do.

I followed him over a low white-washed railroad fence and we walked back a hundred yards along the road under Doctor Eckleburg's persistent stare. The only building in sight was a small block of yellow brick sitting on the edge of the waste land, a sort of compact Main Street ministering to it and contiguous to absolutely nothing. One of the three shops it contained was for rent and another was an all-night restaurant approached by a trail of ashes; the third was a garage—Repairs. GEORGE B. WILSON. Cars Bought and Sold—and I followed Tom inside.

The interior was unprosperous and bare; the only car visible was the dust-covered wreck of a Ford which crouched in a dim corner. It had occurred to me that this shadow of a garage must be a blind and that sumptuous and romantic apartments were concealed overhead when the proprietor himself appeared in the door of an office, wiping his hands on a piece of waste. He was a blonde, spiritless man, anæmic and faintly handsome. When he saw us a damp gleam of hope sprang into his light blue eyes.

"Hello Wilson, old man," said Tom, slapping him jovially on the shoulder. "How's business?"

"I can't complain," answered Wilson unconvincingly. "When are you going to sell me that car?"

"Next week; I've got my man working on it now."

"Works pretty slow, don't he?"

"No, he doesn't," said Tom coldly. "And if you feel that way about it maybe I'd better sell it somewhere else after all."

"I don't mean that," explained Wilson quickly. "I just meant——"

His voice faded off and Tom glanced impatiently around the garage. Then I heard footsteps on a stairs and in a moment the thickish figure of a woman blocked out the light from the office door. She was in the middle thirties, and faintly stout, but she carried her surplus flesh sensuously as some women can. Her face, above a spotted dress of dark blue crêpe-de-chine, contained no facet or gleam of beauty but there was an immediately perceptible vitality about her as if the nerves of her body were continually smouldering. She smiled slowly and walking through her husband as if he were a ghost shook hands with Tom, looking him flush in the eye. Then she wet her lips and without turning around spoke to her husband in a soft, coarse voice:

"Get some chairs, why don't you, so somebody can sit down."

"Oh sure," agreed Wilson hurriedly and went toward the little office, mingling immediately with the cement color of the walls. A white ashen dust veiled his dark suit and his pale hair as it veiled everything in the vicinity—except his wife, who moved close to Tom.

"I want to see you," said Tom intently. "Get on the next train."

"All right."

"I'll meet you by the news-stand on the lower level."

She nodded and moved away from him just as George Wilson emerged with two chairs from his office door.

We waited for her down the road and out of sight. It was a few days before the Fourth of July, and a grey, scrawny Italian child was setting torpedoes in a row along the rail-road track.

"Terrible place, isn't it," said Tom, exchanging a frown with Doctor Eckleburg.

"Awful."

"It does her good to get away."

"Doesn't her husband object?"

"Wilson? He thinks she goes to see her sister in New York. He's so dumb he doesn't know he's alive."

So Tom Buchanan and his girl and I went up together to New York—or not quite together, for Mrs. Wilson sat discreetly in another car. Tom deferred that much to the sensibilities of those East Eggers who might be on the train.

She had changed her dress to a brown figured muslin which stretched tight over her rather wide hips as Tom helped her to the platform in New York. At the news-stand she bought a copy of "Town Tattle" and a moving picture magazine and, in the station drug store, some cold cream and a small flask of perfume. Upstairs in the solemn echoing drive she let four taxi cabs drive away before she selected a new one, lavender-colored with grey upholstery, and in this we slid out from the mass of the station into the glowing sunshine. But immediately she turned sharply from the window and leaning forward tapped on the front glass.

"I want to get one of those dogs," she said earnestly. "I want to get one for the apartment. They're nice to have—a dog."

We backed up to a grey old man who bore an absurd resemblance to John D. Rockefeller. In a basket, swung from his neck, cowered a dozen very recent puppies of an indeterminate breed.

"What kind are they?" asked Mrs. Wilson eagerly as he came to the taxi window.

"All kinds. What kind do you want, lady?"

"I'd like to get one of those police dogs; I don't suppose you got that kind?"

The man peered doubtfully into the basket, plunged in his hand and drew one up, wriggling, by the back of the neck.

"That's no police dog," said Tom.

"No, it's not exactly a pol*ice* dog," said the man with

disappointment in his voice. "It's more of an airedale." He passed his hand over the brown washrag of a back. "Look at that coat. Some coat. That's a dog that'll never bother you with catching cold."

"I think it's cute," said Mrs. Wilson enthusiastically. "How much is it?"

"That dog?" He looked at it admiringly. "That dog will cost you ten dollars."

The airedale—undoubtedly there was an airedale concerned in it somewhere though its feet were startlingly white—changed hands and settled down into Mrs. Wilson's lap where she fondled the weather-proof coat with rapture.

"Is it a boy or a girl?" she asked delicately.

"That dog? That dog's a boy."

"It's a bitch," said Tom decisively. "Here's your money. Go and buy ten more dogs with it."

We drove over to Fifth Avenue, so warm and soft, almost pastoral, on the summer Sunday afternoon that I wouldn't have been surprised to see a great flock of white sheep turn the corner.

"Hold on," I said. "I have to leave you here."

"No, you don't," interposed Tom quickly. "Myrtle'll be hurt if you don't come up to the apartment. Won't you, Myrtle?"

"Come on," she urged. "I'll telephone my sister Catherine. She's said to be very beautiful by people who ought to know."

"Well, I'd like to, but——"

We went on, cutting back again over the Park toward the West Hundreds. At 158th Street the cab stopped at one slice in a long white cake of apartment houses. Throwing a regal homecoming glance around the neighborhood, Mrs. Wilson gathered up her dog and her other purchases and went haughtily in.

"I'm going to have the McKees come up," she announced as we rose in the elevator. "And of course I got to call up my sister too."

The apartment was on the top floor—a small living room, a small dining room, a small bedroom and a bath. The living room was crowded to the doors with a set of tapestried furniture entirely too large for it so that to move about was to stumble continually over scenes of ladies swinging in the gardens of Versailles. The only picture was an over-enlarged photograph, apparently a hen sitting on a blurred rock. Looked at from a distance however the hen resolved itself into a bonnet and the countenance of a stout old lady beamed down into the room. Several old copies of "Town Tattle" lay on the table together with a copy of "Simon Called Peter" and some of the small scandal magazines of Broadway. Mrs. Wilson was first concerned with the dog. A reluctant elevator boy went for a box full of straw and some milk to which he added on his own initiative a tin of large hard dog biscuits—one of which decomposed apathetically in the saucer of milk all afternoon. Meanwhile Tom brought out a bottle of whiskey from a locked bureau door.

I have been drunk just twice in my life and the second time was that afternoon, so everything that happened has a dim hazy cast over it although until after eight o'clock the apartment was full of cheerful sun. Sitting on Tom's lap Mrs. Wilson called up several people on the telephone; then there were no cigarettes and I went out to buy some at the drug store on the corner. When I came back they had disappeared so I sat down discreetly in the living room and read a chapter of "Simon Called Peter"—either it was terrible stuff or the whiskey distorted things because it didn't make any sense to me.

Just as Tom and Myrtle—after the first drink Mrs. Wilson and I called each other by our first names—reappeared, company commenced to arrive at the apartment door.

The sister, Catherine, was a slender, worldly girl of about thirty with a solid sticky bob of red hair and a complexion powdered milky white. Her eyebrows had been plucked and then drawn on again at a more rakish angle but the efforts of nature toward the restoration of the old alignment gave a blurred air to her face. When she moved about there was an incessant clicking as innumerable pottery bracelets jingled up and down upon her arms. She came in with such a proprietary haste and looked around so possessively at the furniture that I wondered if she lived here. But when I asked her she laughed immoderately, repeated my question aloud and told me she lived with a girl friend at a hotel.

Mr. McKee was a pale feminine man from the flat below. He had just shaved for there was a white spot of lather on his cheekbone and he was most respectful in his greeting to everyone in the room. He informed me that he was in the "artistic game" and I gathered later that he was a photographer and had made the dim enlargement of Mrs. Wilson's mother which hovered like an ectoplasm on the wall. His wife was shrill, languid, handsome and horrible. She told me with pride that her husband had photographed her a hundred and twenty-seven times since they had been married.

Mrs. Wilson had changed her costume some time before and was now attired in an elaborate afternoon dress of cream colored chiffon which gave out a continual rustle as she swept about the room. With the influence of the dress her personality had also undergone a change. The intense vitality that had been so remarkable in the garage was converted into impressive hauteur. Her laughter, her gestures, her assertions became more violently affected moment by moment and as she expanded the room grew smaller around her until she seemed to be revolving on a noisy, creaking pivot through the smoky air.

"My dear," she told her sister in a high mincing shout, "most of these fellas will cheat you every time. All they think of is money. I had a woman up here last week to look at my feet and when she gave me the bill you'd of thought she had my appendicitus out."

"What was the name of the woman?" asked Mrs. McKee.

"Mrs. Eberhardt. She goes around looking at people's feet in their own homes."

"I like your dress," remarked Mrs. McKee. "I think it's adorable."

Mrs. Wilson rejected the compliment by raising her eyebrow in disdain.

"It's just a crazy old thing," she said. "I just slip it on sometimes when I don't care what I look like."

"But it looks wonderful on you, if you know what I mean," pursued Mrs. McKee. "If Chester could only get you in that pose I think he could make something of it."

We all looked in silence at Mrs. Wilson who removed a strand of hair from over her eyes and looked back at us with a brilliant smile. Mr. McKee regarded her intently with his head on one side and then moved his hand back and forth slowly in front of his face.

"I should change the light," he said after a moment. "I'd like to bring out the modelling of the features. And I'd try to get hold of all the back hair."

"I wouldn't think of changing the light," cried Mrs. McKee. "I think it's——"

Her husband said "*Sh!*" and we all looked at the subject again whereupon Tom Buchanan yawned audibly and got to his feet.

"You McKees have something to drink," he said. "Get some more ice and mineral water, Myrtle, before everybody goes to sleep."

"I told that boy about the ice." Myrtle raised her eyebrows in despair at the shiftlessness of the lower orders. "These people! You have to keep after them all the time."

She looked at me and laughed pointlessly. Then she flounced over to the dog, kissed it with ecstasy and swept into the kitchen, implying that a dozen chefs awaited her orders there.

"I've done some nice things out on Long Island," asserted Mr. McKee.

Tom looked at him blankly.

"Two of them we have framed downstairs."

"Two what?" demanded Tom.

"Two studies. One of them I call 'Montauk Point—the Gulls,' and the other I call 'Montauk Point—the Sea.' "

The sister Catherine sat down beside me on the couch.

"Do you live down on Long Island too?" she inquired.

"I live at West Egg."

"Really? I was down there at a party about a month ago.

At a man named Gatsby's. Do you know him?"

"I live next door to him."

"Well, they say he's a nephew or a cousin of Kaiser Wilhelm's. That's where all his money comes from."

"Really?"

She nodded.

"I'm scared of him. I'd hate to have him get anything on me."

This absorbing information about my neighbor was interrupted by Mrs. McKee's pointing suddenly at Catherine:

"Chester, I think you could do something with *her*," she broke out, but Mr. McKee only nodded in a bored way and turned his attention to Tom.

"I'd like to do more work on Long Island if I could get the entry. All I ask is that they should give me a start."

"Ask Myrtle," said Tom breaking into a short shout of laughter as Mrs. Wilson entered with a tray. "She'll give you a letter of introduction, won't you, Myrtle?"

"Do what?" she asked startled.

"You'll give McKee a letter of introduction to your husband, so he can do some studies of him." His lips moved silently for a moment as he invented. " 'George B. Wilson at the Gasoline Pump,' or something like that."

Catherine leaned close to me and whispered in my ear:

"Neither of them can stand the person they're married to."

"Can't they?"

"Can't *stand* them." She looked at Myrtle and then at Tom. "What I say is, why go on living with them if they can't stand them? If I was them I'd get a divorce and get married to each other right away."

"Doesn't she like Wilson either?"

The answer to this was unexpected. It came from Myrtle who had overheard the question and it was violent and obscene.

"You see?" cried Catherine triumphantly. She lowered her voice again. "It's really his wife that's keeping them apart. She's a Catholic and they don't believe in divorce."

Daisy was not a Catholic and I was a little shocked at the elaborateness of the lie.

"When they do get married," continued Catherine, "they're going west to live for a while until it blows over."

"It'd be more discreet to go to Europe."

"Oh, do you like Europe?" she exclaimed surprisingly. "I just got back from Monte Carlo."

"Really."

"Just last year. I went over there with another girl."

"Stay long?"

"No, we just went to Monte Carlo and back. We went by way of Marseilles. We had over twelve hundred dollars when we started but we got gypped out of it all in two days in the private rooms. We had an awful time getting back, I can tell you. God, how I hated that town!"

The late afternoon sky bloomed in the window for a moment like the blue honey of the Mediterranean—then the shrill voice of Mrs. McKee called me back into the room.

"I almost made a mistake too," she declared vigorously. "I almost married a little kyke who'd been after me for years. I knew he was below me. Everybody kept saying to me, 'Lucille, that man's way below you!' But if I hadn't met Chester he'd of got me sure."

"Yes, but listen," said Myrtle Wilson, nodding her head

up and down. "At least you didn't marry him."

"I know I didn't."

"Well, I married him," said Myrtle ambiguously. "And that's the difference between your case and mine."

"Why did you, Myrtle?" demanded Catherine. "Nobody forced you to."

Myrtle considered.

"I married him because I thought he was a gentleman," she said finally. "I thought he knew something about breeding but he wasn't fit to lick my shoe."

"You were crazy about him for a while," said Catherine.

"Crazy about him!" cried Myrtle incredulously. "Who said I was crazy about him? I never was any more crazy about him than I was about that man there."

She pointed suddenly at me and everyone looked at me accusingly. I tried to show by my expression that I had played no part in her past.

"The only *crazy* I was was when I married him. I knew right away I made a mistake. He borrowed somebody's best suit to get married in and never even told me about it, and the man came after it one day when he was out." She looked around to see who was listening: " 'Oh, is that your suit?' I said. 'This is the first I ever heard about it.' But I gave it to him and then I lay down and cried to beat the band all afternoon."

"She really ought to get away from him," resumed Catherine to me. "They've been living over that garage for eleven years. And Tom's the first sweetie she ever had."

The bottle of whiskey—a second one—was now in constant demand by all present, excepting Catherine who "felt just as good on nothing at all." Tom rang for the janitor and sent him for some celebrated sandwiches which were a complete supper in themselves. I wanted to get out and walk eastward toward the park through the soft twilight but each time I tried to go I became entangled in some wild strident argument which pulled me back, as if with ropes, into my chair. Yet high over the city our line of yellow windows must have contributed their share of human secrecy to the casual watcher in the darkening streets, and I was him too, looking up and wondering. I was within and without, simultaneously enchanted and repelled by the inexhaustible variety of life.

Myrtle pulled her chair close to mine and suddenly her warm breath poured over me the story of her first meeting with Tom.

"It was on the two little seats facing each other that are always the last ones left on the train. I was going up to New York to see my sister and spend the night. He had on a dress suit and patent leather shoes and I couldn't keep my eyes off him but every time he looked at me I had to pretend to be looking at the advertisement over his head. When we came into the station he was next to me and his white shirt front pressed against my arm—and so I told him I'd have to call a policeman but he knew I lied. I was so excited that when I got into a taxi with him I didn't hardly know I wasn't getting into a subway train. All I kept thinking about over and over was 'You can't live forever, you can't live forever.'"

She turned to Mrs. McKee and the room rang full of her artificial laughter.

"My dear," she cried, "I'm going to give you this dress as soon as I'm through with it. I've got to get another one tomorrow. I'm going to make a list of all the things I've got to get. A massage and a wave and a collar for the dog and one of those cute little ash trays where you touch a spring, and a wreath with a black silk bow for mother's grave that'll last all summer. I got to write down a list so I won't forget all the things I got to do."

It was nine o'clock—almost immediately afterwards I looked at my watch and found it was ten. Mr. McKee was asleep on a chair with his fists clenched in his lap, like a photograph of a man of action. Taking out my handkerchief I wiped from his cheek the remains of the spot of dried lather that had worried me all the afternoon.

The little dog was sitting on the table looking with blind eyes through the smoke and from time to time groaning faintly. People disappeared, reappeared, made plans to go somewhere, and then lost each other, searched for each other, found each other a few feet away. Some time toward midnight Tom Buchanan and Mrs. Wilson stood face to face discussing in impassioned voices whether Mrs. Wilson had any right to mention Daisy's name.

"Daisy! Daisy! Daisy!" shouted Mrs. Wilson. "I'll say it whenever I want to! Daisy! Dai——"

Making a short deft movement Tom Buchanan broke her nose with his open hand.

Then there were bloody towels upon the bathroom floor and women's voices scolding, and high over the confusion a long broken wail of pain. Mr. McKee awoke from his doze and started in a daze toward the door. When he had gone half way he turned around and stared at the scene—his wife and Catherine scolding and consoling as they stumbled here and there among the crowded furniture with articles of aid, and the despairing figure on the couch bleeding fluently and trying to spread a copy of "Town Tattle" over the tapestry scenes of Versailles. Then Mr. McKee turned and continued on out the door. Taking my hat from the chandelier I followed.

"Come to lunch some day," he suggested as we groaned down in the elevator.

"Where?"

"Anywhere."

"Keep your hands off the lever," snapped the elevator boy.

"I beg your pardon," said Mr. McKee with dignity. "I didn't know I was touching it."

"All right," I agreed, "I'll be glad to."

. . . I was standing beside his bed and he was sitting up between the sheets, clad in his underwear, with a great portfolio in his hands.

"Beauty and the Beast . . . Loneliness . . . Old Grocery Horse . . . Brook'n Bridge. . . ."

Then I was lying half asleep in the cold lower level of the Pennsylvania Station, staring at the morning "Tribune" and waiting for the four o'clock train.

CHAPTER III

♦

There was music from my neighbor's house through the summer nights. In his blue gardens men and girls came and went like moths among the whisperings and the champagne and the stars. At high tide in the afternoon I watched his guests diving from the tower of his raft or taking the sun on the hot sand of his beach while his two motor boats slit the waters of the Sound, drawing aquaplanes over cataracts of foam. On week-ends his Rolls-Royce became an omnibus, bearing parties to and from the city, between nine in the morning and long past midnight, while his station wagon scampered like a brisk yellow bug to meet all trains. And on Mondays eight servants including an extra gardener toiled all day with mops and scrubbing-brushes and hammers and garden shears, repairing the ravages of the night before.

Every Friday five crates of oranges and lemons arrived from a fruiterer in New York—every Monday these same oranges and lemons left his back door in a pyramid of pulpless halves. There was a machine in the kitchen which could extract the juice of two hundred oranges in half an hour, if a little button was pressed two hundred times by a butler's thumb.

At least once a fortnight a corps of caterers came down with several hundred feet of canvas and enough colored lights to make a Christmas tree of Gatsby's enormous garden. On buffet tables, garnished with glistening hors d'œuvre, spiced baked hams crowded against salads of harlequin designs and pastry pigs and turkeys bewitched to a dark gold. In the main hall a bar with a real brass rail was set up, and stocked with gins and liquors and with cordials so long forgotten that most of his female guests were too young to know one from another.

By seven o'clock the orchestra has arrived—no thin five piece affair but a whole pit full of oboes and trombones and saxophones and viols and cornets and piccolos and low and high drums. The last swimmers have come in from the beach now and are dressing upstairs; the cars from New York are parked five deep in the drive, and already the halls and salons and verandas are gaudy with primary colors and hair shorn in strange new ways and shawls beyond the dreams of Castile. The bar is in full swing and floating rounds of cocktails permeate the garden outside until the air is alive with chatter and laughter and casual innuendo and introductions forgotten on the spot and enthusiastic meetings between women who never knew each other's names.

The lights grow brighter as the earth lurches away from the sun and now the orchestra is playing yellow cocktail music and the opera of voices pitches a key higher. Laughter is easier, minute by minute, spilled with prodigality, tipped out at a cheerful word. The groups change more swiftly, swell with new arrivals, dissolve and form in the same breath—already there are wanderers, confident girls who weave here and there among the stouter and more stable, become for a sharp, joyous moment the center of a group and then excited with triumph glide on through the sea-change of faces and voices and color under the constantly changing light.

Suddenly one of these gypsies in trembling opal seizes a cocktail out of the air, dumps it down for courage and moving her hands like Frisco dances out alone on the canvas platform. A momentary hush; the orchestra leader varies his rhythm obligingly for her and there is a burst of chatter as the erroneous news goes around that she is Gilda Gray's understudy from the "Follies." The party has begun.

I believe that on the first night I went to Gatsby's house I was one of the few guests who had actually been invited. People were not invited—they went there. They got into automobiles which bore them out to Long Island and some-how they ended up at Gatsby's door. Once there they were introduced by somebody who knew Gatsby and after that they conducted themselves according to the rules of behavior associated with amusement parks. Sometimes they came and went without having met Gatsby at all, came for the party with a simplicity of heart that was its own ticket of admission.

I had been actually invited. A chauffeur in a uniform of robin's egg blue crossed my lawn early that Saturday morning with a surprisingly formal note from his employer—the honor would be entirely Gatsby's, it said, if I would attend his "little party" that night. He had seen me several times and had intended to call on me long before but a peculiar combination of circumstances had prevented it—signed Jay Gatsby in a majestic hand.

Dressed up in white flannels I went over to his lawn a little after seven and wandered around rather ill-at-ease among swirls and eddies of people I didn't know—though here and there was a face I had noticed on the commuting train. I was immediately struck by the number of young Englishmen dotted about; all well dressed, all looking a little hungry and all talking in low earnest voices to solid and prosperous Americans. I was sure that they were all selling something: bonds or insurance or automobiles. They were, at least, agonizingly aware of the easy money in the vicinity and convinced that it was theirs for a few words in the right key.

As soon as I arrived I made an attempt to find my host but the two or three people of whom I asked his whereabouts stared at me in such an amazed way and denied so vehemently any knowledge of his movements that I slunk off in the direction of the cocktail table—the only place in the garden where a single man could linger without looking purposeless and alone.

I was on my way to get roaring drunk from sheer embarrassment when Jordan Baker came out of the house and stood at the head of the marble steps, leaning a little backward and looking with contemptuous interest down into the garden.

Welcome or not, I found it necessary to attach myself to someone before I should begin to address cordial remarks to the passers-by.

"Hello!" I roared, advancing toward her. My voice

seemed unnaturally loud across the garden.

"I thought you might be here," she responded absently as I came up. "I remembered you lived next door to——"

She held my hand impersonally, as a promise that she'd take care of me in a minute, and gave ear to two girls in twin yellow dresses who stopped at the foot of the steps.

"Hello!" they cried together. "Sorry you didn't win."

That was for the golf tournament. She had lost in the finals the week before.

"You don't know who we are," said one of the girls in yellow, "but we met you here about a month ago."

"You've dyed your hair since then," remarked Jordan and I started but the girls had moved casually on and her remark was addressed to the premature moon, produced like the supper, no doubt, out of a caterer's basket. With Jordan's slender golden arm resting in mine we descended the steps and sauntered about the garden. A tray of cocktails floated at us through the twilight and we sat down at a table with the two girls in yellow and three men, each one introduced to us as Mr. Mumble.

"Do you come to these parties often?" inquired Jordan of the girl beside her.

"The last one was the one I met you at," answered the girl in an alert, confident voice. She turned to her companion: "Wasn't it for you, Lucille?"

It was for Lucille too.

"I like to come," Lucille said. "I never care what I do, so I always have a good time. When I was here last I tore my gown on a chair, and he asked me my name and address—inside of a week I got a package from Croirier's with a new evening gown in it."

"Did you keep it?" asked Jordan.

"Sure I did. I was going to wear it tonight, but it was too big in the bust and had to be altered. It was gas blue with lavender beads. Two hundred and sixty-five dollars."

"There's something funny about a fellow that'll do a thing like that," said the other girl eagerly. "He doesn't want any trouble with *any*body."

"Who doesn't?" I inquired.

"Gatsby. Somebody told me——"

The two girls and Jordan leaned together confidentially.

"Somebody told me they thought he killed a man once."

A thrill passed over all of us. The three Mr. Mumbles bent forward and listened eagerly.

"I don't think it's so much *that*," argued Lucille skeptically; "it's more that he was a German spy during the war."

One of the men nodded in confirmation.

"I heard that from a man who knew all about him, grew up with him in Germany," he assured us positively.

"Oh no," said the first girl, "it couldn't be that, because he was in the American army during the war." As our credulity switched back to her she leaned forward with enthusiasm. "You look at him sometime when he thinks nobody's looking at him. I'll bet he killed a man."

She narrowed her eyes and shivered. Lucille shivered. We all turned and looked around for Gatsby. It was testimony to the romantic speculation he inspired that there were whispers about him from those who had found little that it was necessary to whisper about in this world.

The first supper—there would be another one after midnight—was now being served and Jordan invited me to join her own party who were spread around a table on the other side of the garden. There were three married couples and Jordan's escort, a persistent undergraduate given to violent innuendo and obviously under the impression that sooner or later Jordan was going to yield him up her person to a greater or lesser degree. Instead of rambling this party had preserved a dignified homogeneity, and assumed to itself the function of representing the staid nobility of the country-side—East Egg condescending to West Egg, and carefully on guard against its spectroscopic gayety.

"Let's get out," whispered Jordan, after a somehow wasteful and inappropriate half hour. "This is much too polite for me."

We got up and she explained that we were going to find the host—I had never met him, she said, and it was making me uneasy. The undergraduate nodded in a cynical, melancholy way.

The bar, where we glanced first, was crowded but Gatsby was not there. She couldn't find him from the top of the steps, and he wasn't on the veranda. On a chance we tried an important-looking door, and walked into a high Gothic library, panelled with carved English oak, and probably transported complete from some ruin overseas.

A stout, middle-aged man with enormous owl-eyed spectacles was sitting somewhat drunk on the edge of a great table, staring with unsteady concentration at the shelves of books. As we entered he wheeled excitedly around and examined Jordan from head to foot.

"What do you think?" he demanded impetuously.

"About what?"

He waved his hand toward the book-shelves.

"About that. As a matter of fact you needn't bother to ascertain. I ascertained. They're real."

"The books?"

He nodded.

"Absolutely real—have pages and everything. I thought they'd be a nice durable cardboard. Matter of fact they're absolutely real. Pages and—— Here! Lemme show you."

Taking our skepticism for granted he rushed to the bookcases and returned with Volume One of the "Stoddard Lectures."

"See!" he cried triumphantly. "It's a bona fide piece of printed matter. It fooled me. This fella's a regular Belasco. It's a triumph. What thoroughness! What realism! Knew when to stop too—didn't cut the pages. But what do you want? What do you expect?"

He snatched the book from me and replaced it hastily on its shelf muttering that if one brick was removed the whole library was liable to collapse.

"Who brought you?" he demanded. "Or did you just come? I was brought. Most people were brought."

Jordan looked at him alertly, cheerfully without answering.

"I was brought by a woman named Roosevelt," he continued. "Mrs. Claud Roosevelt. Do you know her? I met her somewhere last night. I've been drunk for about a week now, and I thought it might sober me up to sit in a library."

"Has it?"

"A little bit, I think. I can't tell yet. I've only been here an hour. Did I tell you about the books? They're real. They're——"

"You told us."

We shook hands with him gravely and went back out-doors.

There was dancing now on the canvas in the garden, old men pushing young girls backward in eternal graceless circles, superior couples holding each other tortuously, fashionably and keeping in the corners—and a great number of single girls dancing individualistically or relieving the orchestra for a moment of the burden of the banjo or the traps. By midnight the hilarity had increased. A celebrated tenor had sung in Italian and a notorious contralto had sung in jazz and between the numbers people were doing "stunts" all over the garden while happy vacuous bursts of laughter rose toward the summer sky. A pair of stage "twins"—who turned out to be the girls in yellow—did a baby act in costume and champagne was served in glasses bigger than finger bowls. The moon had risen higher, and floating in the Sound was a triangle of silver scales, trembling a little to the stiff, tinny drip of the banjoes on the lawn.

I was still with Jordan Baker. We were sitting at a table with a man of about my age and a rowdy little girl who gave way upon the slightest provocation to uncontrollable laughter. I was enjoying myself now. I had taken two finger bowls of champagne and the scene had changed before my eyes into something significant, elemental and profound.

At a lull in the entertainment the man looked at me and smiled.

"Your face is familiar," he said politely. "Weren't you in the Third Division during the war?"

"Why, yes. I was in the Ninth Machine-Gun Battalion."

"I was in the Seventh Infantry until June nineteen-eighteen. I knew I'd seen you somewhere before."

We talked for a moment about some wet, grey little villages in France. Evidently he lived in this vicinity for he told me that he had just bought a hydroplane and was going to try it out in the morning.

"Want to go with me, old sport? Just near the shore along the Sound."

"What time?"

"Any time that suits you best."

It was on the tip of my tongue to ask his name when Jordan looked around and smiled.

"Having a gay time now?" she inquired.

"Much better." I turned again to my new acquaintance. "This is an unusual party for me. I haven't even seen the host. I live over there——" I waved my hand at the invisible hedge in the distance, "and this man Gatsby sent over his chauffeur with an invitation."

For a moment he looked at me as if he failed to understand.

"I'm Gatsby," he said suddenly.

"What!" I exclaimed. "Oh, I beg your pardon."

"I thought you knew, old sport. I'm afraid I'm not a very good host."

He smiled understandingly—much more than understandingly. It was one of those rare smiles with a quality of eternal reassurance in it, that you may come across four or five times in life. It faced—or seemed to face—the whole external world for an instant, and then concentrated on *you* with an irresistible prejudice in your favor. It understood you just so far as you wanted to be understood, believed in you as you would like to believe in yourself and assured you that it had precisely the impression of you that, at your best, you hoped to convey. Precisely at that point it vanished— and I was looking at an elegant young rough-neck, a year or two over thirty, whose elaborate formality of speech just missed being absurd. Some time before he introduced himself I'd got a strong impression that he was picking his words with care.

Almost at the moment when Mr. Gatsby identified himself a butler hurried toward him with the information that Chicago was calling him on the wire. He excused himself with a small bow that included each of us in turn.

"If you want anything just ask for it, old sport," he urged me. "Excuse me. I will rejoin you later."

When he was gone I turned immediately to Jordan— constrained to assure her of my surprise. I had expected that Mr. Gatsby would be a florid and corpulent person in his middle years.

"Who is he?" I demanded. "Do you know?"

"He's just a man named Gatsby."

"Where is he from, I mean? And what does he do?"

"Now *you*'re started on the subject," she answered with a wan smile. "Well,—he told me once he was an Oxford man."

A dim background started to take shape behind him but at her next remark it faded away.

"However, I don't believe it."

"Why not?"

"I don't know," she insisted. "I just don't think he went there."

Something in her tone reminded me of the other girl's "I

think he killed a man," and had the effect of stimulating my curiosity. I would have accepted without question the information that Gatsby sprang from the swamps of Louisiana or from the lower East Side of New York. That was comprehensible. But young men didn't—at least in my provincial inexperience I believed they didn't—drift coolly out of nowhere and buy a palace on Long Island Sound.

"Anyhow he gives large parties," said Jordan, changing the subject with an urban distaste for the concrete. "And I like large parties. They're so intimate. At small parties there isn't any privacy."

There was the boom of a bass drum, and the voice of the orchestra leader rang out suddenly above the echolalia of the garden.

"Ladies and gentlemen," he cried. "At the request of Mr. Gatsby we are going to play for you Mr. Vladimir Tostoff's latest work which attracted so much attention at Carnegie Hall last May. If you read the papers you know there was a big sensation." He smiled with jovial condescension and added "Some sensation!" whereupon everybody laughed.

"The piece is known," he concluded lustily, "as 'Vladimir Tostoff's Jazz History of the World.' "

The nature of Mr. Tostoff's composition eluded me, because just as it began my eyes fell on Gatsby, standing alone on the marble steps and looking from one group to another with approving eyes. His tanned skin was drawn attractively tight on his face and his short hair looked as though it were trimmed every day. I could see nothing sinister about him. I wondered if the fact that he was not drinking helped to set him off from his guests, for it seemed to me that he grew more correct as the fraternal hilarity increased. When the "Jazz History of the World" was over girls were putting their heads on men's shoulders in a puppyish, convivial way, girls were swooning backward playfully into men's arms, even into groups knowing that someone would arrest their falls—but no one swooned backward on Gatsby and no French bob touched Gatsby's shoulder and no singing quartets were formed with Gatsby's head for one link.

"I beg your pardon."

Gatsby's butler was suddenly standing beside us.

"Miss Baker?" he inquired. "I beg your pardon but Mr. Gatsby would like to speak to you alone."

"With me?" she exclaimed in surprise.

"Yes, madame."

She got up slowly, raising her eyebrows at me in astonishment, and followed the butler toward the house. I noticed that she wore her evening dress, all her dresses, like sports clothes—there was a jauntiness about her movements as if she had first learned to walk upon golf courses on clean, crisp mornings.

I was alone and it was almost two. For some time confused and intriguing sounds had issued from a long many-windowed room which overhung the terrace. Eluding Jordan's undergraduate who was now engaged in an obstetrical conversation with two chorus girls and who implored me to join him, I went inside.

The large room was full of people. One of the girls in yellow was playing the piano and beside her stood a tall red haired young lady from a famous chorus, engaged in song. She had drunk a quantity of champagne and during the course of her song she had decided ineptly that everything was very very sad—she was not only singing, she was weeping too. Whenever there was a pause in the song she filled it with gasping broken sobs and then took up the lyric again in a quavering soprano. The tears coursed down her cheeks—not freely, however, for when they came into contact with her heavily beaded eyelashes they assumed an inky color, and pursued the rest of their way in slow black rivulets. A humorous suggestion was made that she sing the notes on her face whereupon she threw up her hands, sank into a chair and went off into a deep vinous sleep.

"She had a fight with a man who says he's her husband," explained a girl at my elbow.

I looked around. Most of the remaining women were now having fights with men said to be their husbands. Even Jordan's party, the quartet from East Egg, were rent asunder by dissension. One of the men was talking with curious intensity to a young actress, and his wife after attempting to laugh at the situation in a dignified and indifferent way broke down entirely and resorted to flank attacks—at intervals she appeared suddenly at his side like an angry diamond and hissed "You promised!" into his ear.

The reluctance to go home was not confined to wayward men. The hall was at present occupied by two deplorably sober men and their highly indignant wives. The wives were sympathizing with each other in slightly raised voices.

"Whenever he sees I'm having a good time he wants to go home."

"Never heard anything so selfish in my life."

"We're always the first ones to leave."

"So are we."

"Well, we're almost the last tonight," said one of the men sheepishly. "The orchestra left half an hour ago."

In spite of the wives' agreement that such malevolence was beyond credibility the dispute ended in a short struggle and both wives were lifted kicking into the night.

As I waited for my hat in the hall the door of the library opened and Jordan Baker and Gatsby came out together. He was saying some last word to her but the eagerness in his manner tightened abruptly into formality as several people approached him to say goodbye.

Jordan's party were calling impatiently to her from the porch but she lingered for a moment to shake hands.

"I've just heard the most amazing thing," she whispered. "How long were we in there?"

"Why,—about an hour."

"It was—simply amazing," she repeated abstractedly. "But I swore I wouldn't tell it and here I am tantalizing you." She yawned gracefully in my face. "Please come and see me. . . . Phone book. . . . Under the name of Mrs. Sigourney Howard. . . . My aunt. . . . " She was hurrying off as she talked—her brown hand waved a jaunty salute as she melted into her party at the door.

Rather ashamed that on my first appearance I had stayed so late, I joined the last of Gatsby's guests who were clustered around him. I wanted to explain that I'd hunted for him early in the evening and to apologize for not having known him in the garden.

"Don't mention it," he enjoined me eagerly. "Don't give it another thought, old sport." The familiar expression held no more familiarity than the hand which reassuringly brushed my shoulder. "And don't forget we're going up in the hydroplane tomorrow morning at nine o'clock."

Then the butler, behind his shoulder:

"Philadelphia wants you on the phone, sir."

"All right, in a minute. Tell them I'll be right there. . . . Good night."

"Good night."

"Good night." He smiled—and suddenly there seemed to be a pleasant significance in having been among the last to go, as if he had desired it so all the time. "Good night, old sport. . . . Good night."

But as I walked down the steps I saw that the evening was not quite over. Fifty feet from the door a dozen headlights illuminated a bizarre and tumultuous scene. In the ditch beside the road, right side up but violently shorn of one wheel, rested a new coupé which had left Gatsby's drive not two minutes before. The sharp jut of a wall accounted for the detachment of the wheel which was now getting considerable attention from half a dozen curious chauffeurs. However, as they had left their cars blocking the road a harsh discordant din from those in the rear had been audible for some time and added to the already violent confusion of the scene.

A man in a long duster had dismounted from the wreck and now stood in the middle of the road looking from the car to the tire and from the tire to the observers in a pleasant puzzled way.

"See!" he explained. "It went in the ditch."

The fact was infinitely astonishing to him—and I recognized first the unusual quality of wonder and then the man—it was the late patron of Gatsby's library.

"How'd it happen?"

He shrugged his shoulders.

"I know nothing whatever about mechanics," he said decisively.

"But how did it happen? Did you run into the wall?"

"Don't ask me," said Owl Eyes, washing his hands of the whole matter. "I know very little about driving—next to nothing. It happened, and that's all I know."

"Well, if you're a poor driver you oughtn't to try driving at night."

"But I wasn't even trying," he explained indignantly. "I wasn't even trying."

An awed hush fell upon the bystanders.

"Do you want to commit suicide?"

"You're lucky it was just a wheel! A bad driver and not even *try*ing!"

"You don't understand," explained the criminal. "I wasn't driving. There's another man in the car."

The shock that followed this declaration found voice in a sustained "Ah-h-h!" as the door of the coupé swung slowly open. The crowd—it was now a crowd—stepped back involuntarily and when the door had opened wide there was a ghostly pause. Then, very gradually, part by part, a pale dangling individual stepped out of the wreck, pawing tentatively at the ground with a large uncertain dancing shoe.

Blinded by the glare of the headlights and confused by the incessant groaning of the horns the apparition stood swaying for a moment before he perceived the man in the duster.

"Wha's matter?" he inquired calmly. "Did we run outa gas?"

"Look!"

Half a dozen fingers pointed at the amputated wheel—he stared at it for a moment and then looked upward as though he suspected that it had dropped from the sky.

"It came off," someone explained.

He nodded.

"At first I din' notice we'd stopped."

A pause. Then taking a long breath and straightening his shoulders he remarked in a determined voice:

"Wonder'ff tell me where there's a gas'line station?"

At least a dozen men, some of them little better off than he was, explained to him that wheel and car were no longer joined by any physical bond.

"Back out," he suggested after a moment. "Put her in reverse."

"But the *wheel's* off!"

He hesitated.

"No harm in trying," he said.

The caterwauling horns had reached a crescendo and I turned away and cut across the lawn toward home. I glanced back once. A wafer of a moon was shining over Gatsby's house, making the night fine as before and surviving the laughter and the sound of his still glowing garden. A sudden emptiness seemed to flow now from the windows and the great doors, endowing with complete isolation the figure of the host who stood on the porch, his hand up in a formal gesture of farewell.

Reading over what I have written so far I see I have given the impression that the events of three nights several weeks apart were all that absorbed me. On the contrary they were merely casual events in a crowded summer and, until much later, they absorbed me infinitely less than my personal affairs.

Most of the time I worked. In the early morning the sun threw my shadow westward as I hurried down the white chasms of lower New York to the Probity Trust. I knew the other clerks and young bond-salesmen by their first names and lunched with them in dark crowded restaurants on little pig sausages and mashed potatoes and coffee. I even had a short affair with a girl who lived in Jersey City and worked in the accounting department but her brother began throwing mean looks in my direction so when she went on her vacation in July I let it blow quietly away.

I took dinner usually at the Yale Club—for some reason it was the gloomiest event of my day—and then I went upstairs to the library and studied investments and securities for a conscientious hour. There were generally a few rioters around but they never came into the library so it was a good place to work. After that if the night was mellow I strolled down Madison Avenue past the old Murray Hill Hotel and over Thirty-third Street to the Pennsylvania Station.

I began to like New York, the racy, adventurous feel of it at night and the satisfaction that the constant flicker of men and women and machines gives to the restless eye. I liked to walk up Fifth Avenue and pick out romantic women from the crowd and imagine that in a few minutes I was going to enter into their lives, and no one would ever know or disapprove. Sometimes, in my mind, I followed them to their apartments on the corners of hidden streets, and they turned and smiled back at me before they faded through a door into warm darkness. At the enchanted metropolitan twilight I felt a haunting loneliness sometimes, and felt it in others—poor young clerks who loitered in front of windows waiting until it was time for a solitary restaurant dinner—young clerks in the dusk, wasting the most poignant moments of night and life.

Again at eight o'clock, when the dark lanes of the Forties were five deep with throbbing taxi cabs, bound for the theatre district, I felt a sinking in my heart. Forms leaned together in the taxis as they waited, and voices sang, and there was laughter from unheard jokes, and lighted cigarettes outlined unintelligible gestures inside. Imagining that I, too, was hurrying toward gayety and sharing their intimate excitement, I wished them well.

For a while I lost sight of Jordan Baker, and then in midsummer I found her again. At first I was flattered to go places with her because she was a golf champion and everyone knew her name. Then it was something more. I wasn't actually in love, but I felt a sort of tender curiosity. The bored haughty face that she turned to the world concealed something—most affectations conceal something eventually, even though they don't in the beginning—and one day I found what it was. When we were on a house party together up in Warwick, she left a borrowed car out in the rain with the top down, and then lied about it—and suddenly I remembered the story about her that had eluded me that night at Daisy's. At her first big golf tournament there was a row that nearly reached the newspapers—a suggestion that she had moved her ball from a bad lie in the semi-final round. The thing approached the proportions of a scandal—then died away. A caddy retracted his statement and the only other witness admitted that he might have been mistaken. The incident and the name had remained together in my mind.

Jordan Baker instinctively avoided clever shrewd men and now I saw that this was because she felt safer on a plane where any divergence from a code would be thought impossible. She was incurably dishonest. She wasn't able to endure being at a disadvantage, and given this unwillingness I suppose she had begun dealing in subterfuges when she was very young in order to keep that cool insolent smile turned to the world and yet satisfy the demands of her hard jaunty body.

It made no difference to me. Dishonesty in a woman is a thing you never blame deeply—I was casually sorry, and then I forgot. It was on that same house party that we had a curious conversation about driving a car. It started because she passed so close to some workmen that our fender flicked a button on one man's coat.

"You're a rotten driver," I protested. "Either you ought to be more careful or you oughtn't to drive at all."

"I am careful."

"No, you're not."

"Well, other people are," she said lightly.

"What's that got to do with it?"

"They'll keep out of my way," she insisted. "It takes two to make an accident."

"Suppose you met somebody just as careless as yourself."

"I hope I never will," she answered. "I hate careless people. That's why I like you."

Her grey sun-strained eyes stared straight ahead, but she had deliberately shifted our relations, and for a moment I thought I loved her. But I am slow thinking and full of interior rules that act as brakes on my desires, and I knew that first I had to get myself definitely out of that tangle back home. I'd been writing letters once a week and signing them "Love, Nick," and all I could think of was how, when that certain girl played tennis, a faint mustache of perspiration appeared on her upper lip. Nevertheless there was a vague understanding that had to be tactfully broken off before I was free.

Everyone suspects himself of at least one of the cardinal virtues, and this is mine: I am one of the few honest people that I have ever known.

CHAPTER IV

♦

On Sunday morning while church bells rang in the villages along shore the world and its mistress returned to Gatsby's house and twinkled hilariously on his lawn.

"He's a bootlegger," said the young ladies, moving somewhere between his cocktails and his flowers. "One time he killed a man who had found out that he was nephew to von Hindenburg and second cousin to the devil. Reach me a rose, honey, and pour me a last drop into that there crystal glass."

Once I wrote down on the empty spaces of a time-table the names of those who came to Gatsby's house that summer. It is an old time-table now, disintegrating at its folds and headed "This schedule in effect July 5th, 1922." But I can still read the grey names and they will give you a better impression than my generalities of those who accepted Gatsby's hospitality and paid him the subtle tribute of knowing nothing whatever about him.

From East Egg, then, came the Chester Beckers and the Leeches and a man named Bunsen whom I knew at Yale and

Doctor Webster Civet who was drowned last summer up in Maine. And the Hornbeams and the Willie Voltaires and a whole clan named Blackbuck who always gathered in a corner and flipped up their noses like goats at whosoever came near. And the Ismays and the Chrysties (or rather Hubert Auerbach and Mr. Chrystie's wife) and Edgar Beaver whose hair they say turned cotton-white one winter afternoon for no good reason at all.

Clarence Endive was from East Egg, as I remember. He came only once, in white knickerbockers, and had a fight with a bum named Etty in the garden. From farther out on the Island came the Cheadles and the O. R. P. Schraeders and the Stonewall Jackson Abrams of Georgia and the Fishguards and the Ripley Snells. Snell was there three days before he went to the penitentiary, so drunk out on the gravel drive that Mrs. Ulysses Swett's automobile ran over his right hand. The Dancies came too and S. B. Whitebait, who was well over sixty, and Maurice A. Flink and the Hammerheads and Beluga the tobacco importer and Beluga's girls.

From West Egg came the Poles and the Mulreadys and Cecil Roebuck and Cecil Schoen and Gulick, the state senator, and Newton Orchid who controlled Films Par Excellence and Eckhaust and Clyde Cohen and Don S. Schwartze (the son) and Arthur McCarty, all connected with the movies in one way or another. And the Catlips and the Bembergs and G. Earl Muldoon, brother to that Muldoon who afterwards strangled his wife. Da Fontano the promoter came there and Ed Legros and James B. ("Rot-gut") Ferret and the de Jongs and Ernest Lilly—they came to gamble and when Ferret wandered into the garden it meant he was cleaned out and Associated Traction would have to fluctuate profitably next day.

A man named Klipspringer was there so often and so long that he became known as "the boarder"—I doubt if he had any other home. Of theatrical people there were Gus Waize and Horace O'Donavan and Lester Myer and George Duckweed and Francis Bull. Also from New York were the Chromes and the Backhyssons and the Dennickers and Russel Betty and the Corrigans and the Kellehers and the Dewars and the Scullys and S. W. Belcher and the Smirkes and the young Quinns, divorced now, and Henry L. Palmetto who killed himself by jumping in front of a subway train in Times Square.

Benny McClenahan arrived always with four girls. They were never quite the same ones in physical person but they were so identical one with another that it inevitably seemed they had been there before. I have forgotten their names—Jaqueline, I think, or else Consuela or Gloria or Judy or June, and their last names were either the melodious names of flowers and months or the sterner ones of the great American capitalists whose cousins, if pressed, they would confess themselves to be.

In addition to all these I can remember that Faustina O'Brien came there at least once and the Baedeker girls and young Brewer who had his nose shot off in the war and Mr. Albrucksburger and Miss Haag, his fiancée, and Ardita Fitz-Peters, and Mr. P. Jewett, once head of the American Legion, and Miss Claudia Hip with a man reputed to be her chauffeur, and a prince of something whom we called Duke and whose name, if I ever knew it, I have forgotten.

All these people came to Gatsby's house in the summer.

At nine o'clock one morning late in July Gatsby's gor-geous car lurched up the rocky drive to my door and gave out a burst of melody from its three noted horn. It was the first time he had called on me though I had gone to two of his parties, mounted in his hydroplane, and, at his urgent invitation, made frequent use of his beach.

"Good morning, old sport. You're having lunch with me today and I thought we'd ride up together."

He was balancing himself on the dashboard of his car with that resourcefulness of movement that is so peculiarly American—that comes, I suppose, with the absence of lift-ing work or rigid sitting in youth and, even more, with the formless grace of our nervous, sporadic games. This quality was continually breaking through his punctilious manner in the shape of restlessness. He was never quite still; there was always a tapping foot somewhere or the impatient opening and closing of a hand.

He saw me looking with admiration at his car.

"It's pretty, isn't it, old sport." He jumped off to give me a better view. "Haven't you ever seen it before?"

I'd seen it. Everybody had seen it. It was a rich cream color, bright with nickel, swollen here and there in its mon-strous length with triumphant hatboxes and supper-boxes and tool-boxes, and terraced with a labyrinth of wind-shields that mirrored a dozen suns. Sitting down behind many layers of glass in a sort of green leather conservatory we started to town.

I had talked with him perhaps half a dozen times in the

past month and found, to my disappointment, that he had little to say. So my first impression, that he was a person of some undefined consequence, had gradually faded and he had become simply the proprietor of an elaborate road-house next door.

And then came that disconcerting ride. We hadn't reached West Egg Village before Gatsby began leaving his elegant sentences unfinished and slapping himself indecisively on the knee of his caramel-colored suit.

"Look here, old sport," he broke out surprisingly. "What's your opinion of me anyhow?"

A little overwhelmed I began the generalized evasions which that question deserves.

"Well, I'm going to tell you something about my life," he interrupted. "I don't want you to get a wrong idea of me from all these stories you hear."

So he was aware of the bizarre accusations that flavored conversation in his halls.

"I'll tell you God's truth." His right hand suddenly ordered divine retribution to stand by. "I am the son of some wealthy people in the middle-west—all dead now. I was brought up in America but educated at Oxford because all my ancestors have been educated there for many years. It is a family tradition."

He looked at me sideways—and I knew why Jordan Baker had believed he was lying. He hurried the phrase "educated at Oxford," or swallowed it or choked on it as though it had bothered him before. And with this doubt his whole statement fell to pieces and I wondered if there wasn't something a little sinister about him after all.

"What part of the middle-west?" I inquired casually.

"San Francisco."

"I see."

"My family all died and I came into a good deal of money."

His voice was solemn as if the memory of that sudden extinction of a clan still haunted him. For a moment I suspected that he was pulling my leg but a glance at him convinced me otherwise.

"After that I lived like a young rajah in all the capitals of Europe—Paris, Venice, Rome—collecting jewels, chiefly rubies, hunting big game, painting a little, things for myself only, and trying to forget something very sad that had happened to me long ago."

With an effort I managed to restrain my incredulous laughter. The very phrases were worn so threadbare that they evoked no image except that of a turbaned "character" leaking sawdust at every pore as he pursued a tiger through the Bois de Boulogne.

"Then came the war, old sport. It was a great relief and I tried very hard to die but I seemed to bear an enchanted life. I accepted a commission as first lieutenant when it began. In the Argonne Forest I took two machine-gun detachments so far forward that there was a half mile gap on either side of us where the infantry couldn't advance. We stayed there two days and two nights, a hundred and thirty men with sixteen Lewis guns, and when the infantry came up at last they found the insignia of three German divisions among the piles of dead. I was promoted to be a major and every Allied government gave me a decoration—even Montenegro, little Montenegro down on the Adriatic Sea!"

Little Montenegro! He lifted up the words and nodded at

them—with his smile. The smile comprehended Montenegro's troubled history and sympathized with the brave struggles of the Montenegrin people. It appreciated fully the chain of national circumstances which had elicited this tribute from Montenegro's warm little heart. My incredulity was submerged in fascination now; it was like skimming hastily through a dozen magazines.

He reached in his pocket and a piece of metal, slung on a ribbon, fell into my palm.

"That's the one from Montenegro."

To my astonishment the thing had an authentic look. *Orderi di Danilo,* ran the circular legend, *Montenegro, Nicolas Rex.*

"Turn it."

Major Jay Gatsby, I read, *For Valour Extraordinary.*

"Here's another thing I always carry. A souvenir of Oxford days. It was taken in Trinity Quad—the man on my left is now the Earl of Doncaster."

It was a photograph of half a dozen young men in blazers loafing in an archway through which were visible a host of spires. There was Gatsby, looking a little, not much, younger—with a cricket bat in his hand.

Then it was all true. I saw the skins of tigers flaming in his palace on the Grand Canal; I saw him opening a chest of rubies to ease, with their crimson-lighted depths, the gnawings of his broken heart.

"I'm going to make a big request of you today," he said, pocketing his souvenirs with satisfaction, "so I thought you ought to know something about me. I didn't want you to think I was just some nobody. You see I usually find myself among strangers because I drift here and there trying to

forget the sad thing that happened to me." He hesitated.
"You'll hear about it this afternoon."

"At lunch?"

"No, this afternoon. I happened to find out that you're
taking Miss Baker to tea."

"Do you mean you're in love with Miss Baker?"

"No, old sport, I'm not. But Miss Baker has kindly con-
sented to speak to you about this matter."

I hadn't the faintest idea what "this matter" was, but I
was more annoyed than interested. I hadn't asked Jordan
to tea in order to discuss Mr. Jay Gatsby. I was sure the
request would be something utterly fantastic and for a
moment I was sorry I'd ever set foot upon his overpopulated
lawn.

He wouldn't say another word. His correctness grew on
him as we neared the city. We passed Port Roosevelt, where
there was a glimpse of red-belted ocean-going ships, and
sped along a cobbled slum lined with the dark, undeserted
saloons of the faded gilt nineteen-hundreds. Then the valley
of ashes opened out on both sides of us, and I had a glimpse
of Mrs. Wilson straining at the garage pump with panting
vitality as we went by.

With fenders spread like wings we scattered light through
half Astoria—only half, for as we twisted among the pillars
of the elevated I heard the familiar "jug-jug-*spat*!" of a
motor cycle, and a frantic policeman rode alongside.

"All right, old sport," called Gatsby. We slowed down.
Taking a white card from his wallet he waved it before the
man's eyes.

"Right you are," agreed the policeman, tipping his cap.
"Know you next time, Mr. Gatsby. Excuse *me*!"

"What was that?" I inquired. "The picture of Oxford?"

"I was able to do the commissioner a favor once, and he sends me a Christmas card every year."

Over the great bridge, with the sunlight through the girders making a constant flicker upon the moving cars, with the city rising up across the river in white heaps and sugar lumps all built with a wish out of non-olfactory money. The city seen from the Queensboro Bridge is always the city seen for the first time, in its first wild promise of all the mystery and the beauty in the world.

A dead man passed us in a hearse heaped with blooms, followed by two carriages with drawn blinds and by more cheerful carriages for friends. The friends looked out at us with the tragic eyes and short upper lips of south-eastern Europe and I was glad that the sight of Gatsby's splendid car was included in their somber holiday. As we crossed Blackwells Island a limousine passed us, driven by a white chauffeur, in which sat three modish Negroes, two bucks and a girl. I laughed aloud as the yolks of their eyeballs rolled toward us in haughty rivalry.

"Anything can happen now that we've slid over this bridge," I thought; "anything at all. . . . "

Even Gatsby could happen, without any particular wonder.

Roaring noon. In a well-fanned Forty-second Street cellar I met Gatsby for lunch. Blinking away the brightness of the street outside my eyes picked him out obscurely in the anteroom, talking to another man.

"Mr. Carraway this is my friend Mr. Wolfshiem."

A small flat-nosed Jew raised his large head and regarded

me with two fine growths of hair which luxuriated in either nostril. After a moment I discovered his tiny eyes in the half darkness.

"—so I took one look at him—" said Mr. Wolfshiem, shaking my hand earnestly, "—and what do you think I did?"

"What?" I inquired politely.

But evidently he was not addressing me for he dropped my hand and covered Gatsby with his expressive nose.

"I handed the money to Katspaugh and I sid, 'All right, Katspaugh, don't pay him a penny till he shuts his mouth.' He shut it then and there."

Gatsby took an arm of each of us and moved forward into the restaurant whereupon Mr. Wolfshiem swallowed a new sentence he was starting and lapsed into a somnambulatory abstraction.

"Highballs?" asked the headwaiter.

"This is a nice restaurant here," said Mr. Wolfshiem looking at the Presbyterian nymphs on the ceiling. "But I like across the street better!"

"Yes, highballs," agreed Gatsby, and then to Mr. Wolfshiem: "It's too hot over there."

"Hot and small—yes," said Mr. Wolfshiem, "but full of memories."

"What place is that?" I asked.

"The old Metropole."

"The old Metropole," brooded Mr. Wolfshiem gloomily. "Filled with faces dead and gone. Filled with friends gone now forever. I can't forget so long as I live the night they shot Rosy Rosenthal there. It was six of us at the table and Rosy had eat and drunk a lot all evening. When it was almost morning the waiter came up to him with a funny look and says somebody wants to speak to him outside. 'All right' says Rosy and begins to get up and I pulled him down in his chair.

" 'Let the bastards come in here if they want you, Rosy, but don't you, so help me, move outside this room.'

"It was four o'clock in the morning then and if we'd of raised the blinds we'd of seen daylight."

"Did he go?" I asked innocently.

"Sure he went,"—Mr. Wolfshiem's nose flashed at me indignantly—"He turned around in the door and says, 'Don't let that waiter take away my coffee!' Then he went out on the sidewalk and they shot him three times in his full belly and drove away."

"Four of them were electrocuted," I said, remembering.

"Five with Becker." His nostrils turned to me in an interested way. "I understand you're looking for a business gonnegtion."

The juxtaposition of these two remarks was startling. Gatsby answered for me.

"Oh, no," he exclaimed, "this isn't the man!"

"No?" Mr. Wolfshiem seemed disappointed.

"This is just a friend. I told you we'd talk about that some other time."

"I beg your pardon," said Mr. Wolfshiem. "I had a wrong man."

A succulent hash arrived and Mr. Wolfshiem, forgetting the more sentimental atmosphere of the old Metropole, began to eat with ferocious delicacy. His eyes, meanwhile, roved very slowly all around the room—he completed the arc by turning to inspect the people directly behind. I think that, except for my presence, he would have taken one short glance beneath our own table.

"Look here, old sport," said Gatsby leaning toward me. "I'm afraid I made you a little angry this morning in the car."

There was the smile again, but this time I held out against it.

"I don't like mysteries," I answered. "And I don't understand why you won't come out frankly and tell me what you want. Why has it all got to come through Miss Baker?"

"Oh, it's nothing underhand," he assured me. "Miss Baker's a great sportswoman, you know, and she'd never do anything that wasn't all right."

Suddenly he looked at his watch, jumped up and hurried from the room leaving me with Mr. Wolfshiem at the table.

"He has to telephone," said Mr. Wolfshiem, following him with his eyes. "Fine fellow, isn't he? Handsome to look at and a perfect gentleman."

"Yes."

"He's an Oggsford man."

"Oh."

"He went to Oggsford College in England. You know Oggsford College?"

"I've heard of it."

"It's one of the most famous colleges in the world."

"Have you known Gatsby for a long time?" I inquired.

"Several years," he answered in a gratified way. "I made the pleasure of his acquaintance just after the war. But I knew I had discovered a man of fine breeding after I talked with him an hour. I said to myself: 'There's the kind of man you'd like to take home and introduce to your mother and sister.' " He paused. "I see you're looking at my cuff buttons."

I hadn't been looking at them, but I did now. They were composed of oddly familiar pieces of ivory.

"Finest specimens of human molars," he informed me.

"Well!" I inspected them. "That's a very interesting idea."

"Yeah." He flipped his sleeves up under his coat. "Yeah, Gatsby's very careful about women. He would never so much as look at a friend's wife."

When the subject of this instinctive trust returned to the table and sat down Mr. Wolfshiem drank his coffee with a jerk and got to his feet.

"I have enjoyed my lunch," he said, "and I'm going to run off from you two young men before I outstay my welcome."

"Don't hurry, Meyer," said Gatsby, without enthusiasm. Mr. Wolfshiem raised his hand in a sort of benediction.

"You're very polite but I belong to another generation," he announced solemnly. "You sit here and discuss your sports and your young ladies and your——" He supplied an imaginary noun with another wave of his hand——"As for me, I am fifty years old, and I won't impose myself on you any longer."

As he shook hands and turned away his tragic nose was trembling. I wondered if I had said anything to offend him.

"He becomes very sentimental sometimes," explained Gatsby. "This is one of his sentimental days. He's quite a character around New York—a denizen of Broadway."

"Who is he anyhow—an actor?"

"No."

"A dentist?"

"Meyer Wolfshiem? No, he's a gambler." Gatsby hesitated, then added coolly: "He's the man who fixed the World's Series back in 1919."

"Fixed the World's Series?" I repeated.

The idea staggered me. I remembered of course that the World's Series had been fixed in 1919 but if I had thought of it at all I would have thought of it as a thing that merely *happened*, the end of some inevitable chain. It never occurred to me that one man could start to play with the faith of fifty million people—with the single-mindedness of a burglar blowing a safe.

"How did he happen to do that?" I asked after a minute.

"He just saw the opportunity."

"Why isn't he in jail?"

"They can't get him, old sport. He's a smart man."

I insisted on paying the check. As the waiter brought my change I caught sight of Tom Buchanan across the crowded room.

"Come along with me for a minute," I said. "I've got to say hello to someone."

When he saw us Tom jumped up and took half a dozen steps in our direction.

"Where've you been?" he demanded eagerly. "Daisy's furious because you haven't called up."

"This is Mr. Gatsby, Mr. Buchanan."

They shook hands briefly and a strained, unfamiliar look of embarrassment came over Gatsby's face.

"How've you been, anyhow?" demanded Tom of me. "How'd you happen to come up this far to eat?"

"I've been having lunch with Mr. Gatsby——"

I turned toward Mr. Gatsby, but he was no longer there.

One October day in nineteen-seventeen—

(said Jordan Baker that afternoon, sitting up very straight on a straight chair in the tea-garden at the Plaza Hotel)

—I was walking along from one place to another half on the sidewalks and half on the lawns. I was happier on the lawns because I had on shoes from England with rubber nobs on the soles that bit into the soft ground. I had on a new plaid skirt also that blew a little in the wind and whenever this happened the red, white and blue banners in front of all the houses stretched out stiff and said *tut-tut-tut-tut* in a disapproving way.

The largest of the banners and the largest of the lawns belonged to Daisy Fay's house. She was just eighteen, two years older than me, and by far the most popular of all the young girls in Louisville. She dressed in white and had a little white roadster and all day long the telephone rang in her house and excited young officers from Camp Taylor demanded the privilege of monopolizing her that night, "anyways for an hour!"

When I came opposite her house that morning her white roadster was beside the curb, and she was sitting in it with a lieutenant I had never seen before. They were so engrossed in each other that she didn't see me until I was five feet away.

"Hello Jordan," she called unexpectedly. "Please come here."

I was flattered that she wanted to speak to me because of

all the older girls I admired her most. She asked me if I was going to the Red Cross and make bandages. I was. Well, then, would I tell them that she couldn't come that day? The officer looked at Daisy while she was speaking, in a way that every young girl wants to be looked at sometime, and because it seemed romantic to me I have remembered the incident ever since. His name was Jay Gatsby and I didn't lay eyes on him again for over four years—even after I'd met him on Long Island I didn't realize it was the same man.

That was nineteen-seventeen. By the next year I had a few beaux myself, and I began to play in tournaments, so I didn't see Daisy very often. She went with a slightly older crowd—when she went with anyone at all. Wild rumors were circulating about her—how her mother had found her packing her bag one winter night to go to New York and say goodbye to a soldier who was going overseas. She was effectually prevented, but she wasn't on speaking terms with her family for several weeks. After that she didn't play around with the soldiers any more but only with a few flat-footed, short-sighted young men in town who couldn't get into the army at all.

By the next autumn she was gay again, gay as ever. She had a début after the Armistice, and in February she was presumably engaged to a man from New Orleans. In June she married Tom Buchanan of Chicago with more pomp and circumstance than Louisville ever knew before. He came down with a hundred people in four private cars and hired a whole floor of the Seelbach Hotel, and the day before the wedding he gave her a string of pearls valued at three hundred and fifty thousand dollars.

I was a bridesmaid. I came into her room half an hour before the bridal dinner and found her lying on her bed as lovely as the June night in her flowered dress—and as drunk as a monkey. She had a bottle of sauterne in one hand and a letter in the other.

" 'Gratulate me," she muttered. "Never had a drink before but oh, how I do enjoy it."

"What's the matter, Daisy?"

I was scared, I can tell you; I'd never seen a girl like that before.

"Here, dearis." She groped around in a waste-basket she had with her on the bed and pulled out the string of pearls. "Take 'em downstairs and give 'em back to whoever they belong to. Tell 'em all Daisy's change' her mine. Say 'Daisy's change' her mine!' "

She began to cry—she cried and cried. I rushed out and found her mother's maid and we locked the door and got her into a cold bath. She wouldn't let go of the letter. She took it into the tub with her and squeezed it up into a wet ball and only let me leave it in the soap dish when she saw that it was coming to pieces like snow.

But she didn't say another word. We gave her spirits of ammonia and put ice on her forehead and hooked her back into her dress and half an hour later when we walked out of the room the pearls were around her neck and the incident was over. Next day at five o'clock she married Tom Buchanan without so much as a shiver and started off on a three months' trip to the South Seas.

I saw them in Santa Barbara when they came back and I thought I'd never seen a girl so mad about her husband.

If he left the room for a minute she'd look around un-
easily and say "Where's Tom gone?" and wear the most
abstracted expression until she saw him coming in the
door. She used to sit on the sand with his head in her lap
by the hour rubbing her fingers over his eyes and looking
at him with unfathomable delight. It was touching to see
them together—it made you laugh in a hushed, fascinated
way. That was in August. A week after I left Santa Barbara Tom ran into a wagon on the Ventura road one
night and ripped a front wheel off his car. The girl who
was with him got into the papers too because her arm
was broken—she was one of the chambermaids in the
Santa Barbara Hotel.

The next April Daisy had her little girl and they went to
France for a year. I saw them one spring in Cannes and
later in Deauville and then they came back to Chicago to
settle down. Daisy was popular in Chicago, as you know.
They moved with a fast crowd, all of them young and rich
and wild, but she came out with an absolutely perfect reputation. Perhaps because she doesn't drink. It's a great advantage not to drink among hard drinking people. You
can hold your tongue and, moreover, you can time any
little irregularity of your own so that everybody else is so
blind that they don't see or care. Perhaps Daisy never went
in for amour at all—and yet there's something in that
voice of hers. . . .

Well, about six weeks ago, she heard the name Gatsby for
the first time in years. It was when I asked you—do you
remember?—if you knew Gatsby in West Egg. After you
had gone home she came into my room and woke me up and
said "What Gatsby?" and when I described him—I was half

asleep—she said in the strangest voice that it must be the man she used to know. It wasn't until then that I connected this Gatsby with the officer in her white car.

When Jordan Baker had finished telling all this we had left the Plaza for half an hour and were driving in a Victoria through Central Park. The sun had gone down behind the tall apartments of the movie stars in the West Fifties and the clear voices of little girls, already gathered like crickets on the grass, rose through the hot twilight:

> *I'm the Sheik of Araby,*
> *Your love belongs to me.*
> *At night when you're asleep,*
> *Into your tent I'll creep——*

"It was a strange coincidence," I said.

"But it wasn't a coincidence at all."

"Why not?"

"Gatsby bought that house so that Daisy would be just across the bay."

Then it had not been merely the stars to which he had aspired on that June night. He came alive to me, delivered suddenly from the womb of his purposeless splendor.

"He wants to know—" continued Jordan "—if you'll invite Daisy to your house some afternoon and then let him come over."

The modesty of the demand shook me. He had waited five years and bought a mansion where he dispensed star-light to casual moths so that he could "come over" some afternoon to a stranger's garden.

"Did I have to know all this before he could ask such a little thing?"

"He's afraid. He's waited so long. He thought you might be offended. You see he's a regular tough underneath it all."

Something worried me.

"Why didn't he ask you to arrange a meeting?"

"He wants her to see his house," she explained. "And your house is right next door."

"Oh!"

"I think he half expected her to wander into one of his parties, some night," went on Jordan, "but she never did. Then he began asking people casually if they knew her, and I was the first one he found. It was that night he sent for me at his dance, and you should have heard the elaborate way he worked up to it. Of course, I immediately suggested a luncheon in New York—and I thought he'd go mad:

" 'I don't want to do anything out of the way!' he kept saying. 'I want to see her right next door.'

"When I said you were a particular friend of Tom's he started to abandon the whole idea. He doesn't know very much about Tom, though he says he's read a Chicago paper for years just on the chance of catching a glimpse of Daisy's name."

It was dark now and as we dipped under a little bridge I put my arm around Jordan's golden shoulder and drew her toward me and asked her to dinner. Suddenly I wasn't thinking of Daisy and Gatsby any more but of this clean, hard, limited person who dealt in universal skepticism and who leaned back jauntily just within the circle of my arm. A phrase began to beat in my ears with a sort of heady excitement: "There are only the pursued, the pursuing, the busy and the tired."

"And Daisy ought to have something in her life," murmured Jordan to me.

"Does she want to see Gatsby?"

"She's not to know about it. Gatsby doesn't want her to know. You're just supposed to invite her to tea."

We passed a barrier of dark trees, and then the façade of Fifty-ninth Street, a block of delicate pale light, beamed down into the Park. Unlike Gatsby and Tom Buchanan I had no girl whose disembodied face floated along the dark cornices and blinding signs and so I drew up the girl beside me, tightening my arms. Her wan scornful mouth smiled and so I drew her up again, closer, this time to my face.

CHAPTER V

♦

When I came home to West Egg that night I was afraid for a moment that my house was on fire. Two o'clock and the whole corner of the peninsula was blazing with light which fell unreal on the shrubbery and made thin elongating glints upon the roadside wires. Turning a corner I saw that it was Gatsby's house, lit from tower to cellar.

At first I thought it was another party, a wild rout that had resolved itself into "hide-and-go-seek" or "sardines-in-the-box" with all the house thrown open to the game. But there wasn't a sound. Only wind in the trees which blew the wires and made the lights go off and on again as if the house had winked into the darkness. As my taxi groaned away I saw Gatsby walking toward me across his lawn.

"Your place looks like the world's fair," I said.

"Does it?" He turned his eyes toward it absently. "I have been glancing into some of the rooms. Let's go to Coney Island, old sport. In my car."

"It's too late."

"Well, suppose we take a plunge in the swimming pool. I haven't made use of it all summer."

"I've got to go to bed."

"All right."

He waited, looking at me with suppressed eagerness.

"I talked with Miss Baker," I said after a moment. "I'm going to call up Daisy tomorrow and invite her over here to tea."

"Oh, that's all right," he said carelessly. "I don't want to put you to any trouble."

"What day would suit you?"

"What day would suit *you*?" he corrected me quickly. "I don't want to put you to any trouble, you see."

"How about the day after tomorrow?"

He considered for a moment. Then, with reluctance:

"I want to get the grass cut," he said.

We both looked at the grass—there was a sharp line where my ragged lawn ended and the darker, well-kept expanse of his began. I suspected that he meant my grass.

"There's another little thing," he said uncertainly, and hesitated.

"Would you rather put it off a few days?" I asked.

"Oh, it isn't about that. At least——" He fumbled with a series of beginnings. "Why, I thought—why, look here, old sport, you don't make much money, do you?"

"Not very much."

This seemed to reassure him and he continued more confidently.

"I thought you didn't, if you'll pardon my—you see, I carry on a little business on the side, a sort of a sideline, you understand. And I thought that if you don't make very much—— You're selling bonds, aren't you, old sport?"

"Trying to."

"Well, this would interest you. It wouldn't take up much of your time and you might pick up a nice bit of money. It happens to be a rather confidential sort of thing."

I realize now that under different circumstances that conversation might have been one of the crises of my life. But, because the offer was obviously and tactlessly for a service to be rendered, I had no choice except to cut him off there.

"I've got my hands full," I said. "I'm much obliged but I couldn't take on any more work."

"You wouldn't have to do any business with Wolfshiem." Evidently he thought that I was shying away from the "gonnegtion" mentioned at lunch, but I assured him he was wrong. He waited a moment longer, hoping I'd begin a conversation, but I was too absorbed to be responsive, so he went unwillingly home.

The evening had made me light-headed and happy; I think I walked into a deep sleep as I entered my front door. So I don't know whether or not Gatsby went to Coney Island or for how many hours he "glanced into rooms" while his house blazed gaudily on. I called up Daisy from the office next morning and invited her to come to tea.

"Don't bring Tom," I warned her.

"What?"

"Don't bring Tom."

"Who is 'Tom'?" she asked innocently.

The day agreed upon was pouring rain. At eleven o'clock a man in a raincoat dragging a lawn-mower tapped at my front door and said that Mr. Gatsby had sent him over to cut my grass. This reminded me that I had forgotten to tell my Finn to come back so I drove into West Egg Village to search for her among soggy white-washed alleys and to buy some cups and lemons and flowers.

The flowers were unnecessary, for at two o'clock a greenhouse arrived from Gatsby's, with innumerable receptacles to contain it. An hour later the front door opened nervously and Gatsby in a white flannel suit, silver shirt and gold colored tie hurried in. He was pale and there were dark signs of sleeplessness beneath his eyes.

"Is everything all right?" he asked immediately.

"The grass looks fine, if that's what you mean."

"What grass?" he inquired blankly. "Oh, the grass in the yard." He looked out the window at it, but judging from his expression I don't believe he saw a thing.

"Looks very good," he remarked vaguely. "One of the papers said they thought the rain would stop about four. I think it was 'The Journal.' Have you got everything you need in the shape of—of tea?"

I took him into the pantry where he looked a little reproachfully at the Finn. Together we scrutinized the twelve lemon cakes from the delicatessen shop.

"Will they do?" I asked.

"Of course, of course! They're fine!" and he added hollowly, " . . . old sport."

The rain cooled about half past three to a damp mist through which occasional thin drops swam like dew. Gatsby looked with vacant eyes through a copy of Clay's "Economics," starting at the Finnish tread that shook the kitchen floor and peering toward the bleared windows from time to time as if a series of invisible but alarming happenings were taking place outside. Finally he got up and informed me in an uncertain voice that he was going home.

"Why's that?"

"Nobody's coming to tea. It's too late!" He looked at his watch as if there was some pressing demand on his time elsewhere. "I can't wait all day."

"Don't be silly; it's just two minutes to four."

He sat down, miserably, as if I had pushed him, and simultaneously there was the sound of a motor turning into my lane. We both jumped up and, a little harrowed myself, I went out into the yard.

Under the dripping bare lilac trees a large open car was coming up the drive. It stopped. Daisy's face, tipped sideways beneath a three-cornered lavender hat, looked out at me with a bright ecstatic smile.

"Is this absolutely where you live, my dearest one?"

The exhilarating ripple of her voice was a wild tonic in the rain. I had to follow the sound of it for a moment, up and down, with my ear alone before any words came through. A damp streak of hair lay like a dash of blue paint across her cheek and her hand was wet with glistening drops as I took it to help her from the car.

"Are you in love with me?" she said low in my ear. "Or why did I have to come alone?"

"That's the secret of Castle Rackrent. Tell your chauffeur to go far away and spend an hour."

"Come back in an hour, Ferdie." Then in a grave murmur, "His name is Ferdie."

"Does the gasoline affect his nose?"

"I don't think so," she said innocently. "Why?"

We went in. To my overwhelming surprise the living room was deserted.

"Well, that's funny!" I exclaimed.

"What's funny?"

She turned her head as there was a light, dignified knocking at the front door. I went out and opened it. Gatsby, pale as death, with his hands plunged like weights in his coat pockets, was standing in a puddle of water glaring tragically into my eyes.

With his hands still in his coat pockets he stalked by me into the hall, turned sharply as if he were on a wire and disappeared into the living room. It wasn't a bit funny. Aware of the loud beating of my own heart I pulled the door to against the increasing rain.

For half a minute there wasn't a sound. Then from the living room I heard a sort of choking murmur and part of a laugh followed by Daisy's voice on a clear artificial note.

"I certainly am awfully glad to see you again."

A pause; it endured horribly. I had nothing to do in the hall so I went into the room.

Gatsby, his hands still in his pockets, was reclining against the mantelpiece in a strained counterfeit of perfect ease, even of boredom. His head leaned back so far that it rested against the face of a defunct mantelpiece clock and from this position his distraught eyes stared down at Daisy who was sitting frightened but graceful on the edge of a stiff chair.

"We've met before," muttered Gatsby. His eyes glanced momentarily at me and his lips parted with an abortive attempt at a laugh. Luckily the clock took this moment to tilt dangerously at the pressure of his head, whereupon he turned and caught it with trembling fingers and set it back in place. Then he sat down, rigidly, his elbow on the arm of the sofa and his chin in his hand.

"I'm sorry about the clock," he said.

My own face had now assumed a deep tropical burn. I couldn't muster up a single commonplace out of the thousand in my head.

"It's an old clock," I told them idiotically.

I think we all believed for a moment that it had smashed in pieces on the floor.

"We haven't met for many years," said Daisy, her voice as matter-of-fact as it could ever be.

"Five years next November."

The automatic quality of Gatsby's answer set us all back at least another minute. I had them both on their feet with the desperate suggestion that they help me make tea in the kitchen when the demoniac Finn brought it in on a tray.

Amid the welcome confusion of cups and cakes a certain physical decency established itself. Gatsby got himself into a shadow and while Daisy and I talked looked conscientiously from one to the other of us with tense unhappy eyes. However, as calmness wasn't an end in itself I made an excuse at the first possible moment and got to my feet.

"Where are you going?" demanded Gatsby in immediate alarm.

"I'll be back."

"I've got to speak to you about something before you go."

He followed me wildly into the kitchen, closed the door and whispered "Oh, God!" in a miserable way.

"What's the matter?"

"This is a terrible mistake," he said, shaking his head from side to side, "a terrible, terrible mistake."

"You're just embarrassed, that's all," and luckily I added: "Daisy's embarrassed too."

"She's embarrassed?" he repeated incredulously.

"Just as much as you are."

"Don't talk so loud."

"You're acting like a little boy," I broke out impatiently. "Not only that but you're rude. Daisy's sitting in there all alone."

He raised his hand to stop my words, looked at me with unforgettable reproach and opening the door cautiously went back into the other room.

I walked out the back way—just as Gatsby had when he had made his nervous circuit of the house half an hour before—and ran for a huge black knotted tree whose massed leaves made a fabric against the rain. Once more it was pouring and my irregular lawn, well-shaved by Gatsby's gardener, abounded in small muddy swamps and prehistoric marshes. There was nothing to look at from under the tree except Gatsby's enormous house so I stared at it, like Kant at his church steeple, for half an hour. A brewer had built it early in the "period" craze, a decade before, and there was a story that he'd agreed to pay five years' taxes on all the neighboring cottages if the owners would have their roofs thatched with straw. Perhaps their refusal took the heart out of his plan to Found a Family—he went into an immediate decline. His children sold his house with the black wreath still on the door. Americans, while occasionally willing to be serfs, have always been obstinate about being peasantry.

After half an hour the sun shone again and the grocer's

automobile rounded Gatsby's drive with the raw material for his servants' dinner—I felt sure he wouldn't eat a spoonful. A maid began opening the upper windows of his house, appeared momentarily in each and, leaning from a large central bay, spat meditatively into the garden. It was time I went back. While the rain continued it had seemed like the murmur of their voices, rising and swelling a little, now and then, with gusts of emotion. But in the new silence I felt that silence had fallen within the house too.

I went in—after making every possible noise in the kitchen short of pushing over the stove—but I don't believe they heard a sound. They were sitting at either end of the couch looking at each other as if some question had been asked or was in the air, and every vestige of embarrassment was gone. Daisy's face was smeared with tears and when I came in she jumped up and began wiping at it with her handkerchief before a mirror. But there was a change in Gatsby that was simply confounding. He literally glowed; without a word or a gesture of exultation a new well-being radiated from him and filled the little room.

"Oh, hello, old sport," he said, as if he hadn't seen me for years. I thought for a moment he was going to shake hands.

"It's stopped raining."

"Has it?" When he realized what I was talking about, that there were twinkle-bells of sunshine in the room, he smiled like a weather man, like an ecstatic patron of recurrent light, and repeated the news to Daisy. "What do you think of that? It's stopped raining."

"I'm glad, Jay." Her throat, full of aching, grieving beauty, told only of her unexpected joy.

"I want you and Daisy to come over to my house," he said. "I'd like to show her around."

"You're sure you want me to come?"

"Absolutely, old sport."

Daisy went upstairs to wash her face—too late I thought with humiliation of my towels—while Gatsby and I waited on the lawn.

"My house looks well, doesn't it?" he demanded. "See how the whole front of it catches the light."

I agreed that it was splendid.

"Yes." His eyes went over it, every arched door and square tower. "It took me just three years to earn the money that bought it."

"I thought you inherited your money."

"I did, old sport," he said automatically, "but I lost most of it in the big panic—the panic of the war."

I think he hardly knew what he was saying, for when I asked him what business he was in he answered "That's my affair," before he realized that it wasn't an appropriate reply.

"Oh, I've been in several things," he corrected himself. "I was in the drug business and then I was in the oil business. But I'm not in either one now." He looked at me with more attention. "Do you mean you've been thinking over what I proposed the other night?"

Before I could answer, Daisy came out of the house and two rows of brass buttons on her dress gleamed in the sunlight.

"That huge place *there?*" she cried pointing.

"Do you like it?"

"I love it, but I don't see how you live there all alone."

"I keep it always full of interesting people, night and day. People who do interesting things. Celebrated people."

Instead of taking the short cut along the Sound we went down to the road and entered by the big postern. With enchanting murmurs Daisy admired this aspect or that of the feudal silhouette against the sky, admired the gardens, the sparkling odor of jonquils and the frothy odor of hawthorn and plum blossoms and the pale gold odor of kiss-me-at-the-gate. It was strange to reach the marble steps and find no stir of bright dresses in and out the door and hear no sound but bird voices in the trees.

And inside as we wandered through Marie Antoinette music rooms and Restoration salons I felt that there were guests concealed behind every couch and table, under orders to be breathlessly silent until we had passed through. As Gatsby closed the door of "the Merton College Library" I could have sworn I heard the owl-eyed man break into ghostly laughter.

We went upstairs, through period bedrooms swathed in rose and lavender silk and vivid with new flowers, through dressing rooms and poolrooms, and bathrooms with sunken baths—intruding into one chamber where a dishevelled man in pajamas was doing liver exercises on the floor. It was Mr. Klipspringer, the "boarder." I had seen him wandering hungrily about the beach that morning. Finally we came to Gatsby's own apartment, a bedroom and a bath and an Adam study, where we sat down and drank a glass of some Chartreuse he took from a cupboard in the wall.

He hadn't once ceased looking at Daisy and I think he revalued everything in his house according to the measure of response it drew from her well-loved eyes. Sometimes, too, he stared around at his possessions in a dazed way as though in her actual and astounding presence none of it was any longer real. Once he nearly toppled down a flight of stairs.

His bedroom was the simplest room of all—except where the dresser was garnished with a toilet set of pure dull gold. Daisy took the brush with delight and smoothed her hair, whereupon Gatsby sat down and shaded his eyes and began to laugh.

"It's the funniest thing, old sport," he said hilariously. "I can't— when I try to——"

He had passed visibly through two states and was entering upon a third. After his embarrassment and his unreasoning joy he was consumed with wonder at her presence. He had been full of the idea so long, dreamed it right through to the end, waited with his teeth set, so to speak, at an inconceivable pitch of intensity. Now, in the reaction, he was running down like an overwound clock.

Recovering himself in a minute he opened for us two hulking patent cabinets which held his massed suits and dressing gowns and ties, and his shirts piled like bricks in stacks a dozen high.

"I've got a man in England who buys me clothes. He sends over a selection of things at the beginning of each season, spring and fall."

He took out a pile of shirts and began throwing them one by one before us, shirts of sheer linen and thick silk and fine flannel which lost their folds as they fell and covered the table in many-colored disarray. While we admired he brought more and the soft rich heap mounted higher— shirts with stripes and scrolls and plaids in coral and apple green and lavender and faint orange with monograms of Indian blue. Suddenly with a strained sound Daisy bent her head into the shirts and began to cry stormily.

"They're such beautiful shirts," she sobbed, her voice muffled in the thick folds. "It makes me sad because I've never seen such—such beautiful shirts before."

After the house we were to see the grounds and the swimming pool and the hydroplane and the midsummer flowers—but outside Gatsby's window it began to rain again so we stood in a row looking at the corrugated surface of the Sound.

"If it wasn't for the mist we could see your home across the bay," said Gatsby. "You always have a green light that burns all night at the end of your dock."

Daisy put her arm through his abruptly but he seemed absorbed in what he had just said. Possibly it had occurred to him that the colossal significance of that light had now vanished forever. Compared to the great distance that had separated him from Daisy it had seemed very near to her, almost touching her. It had seemed as close as a star to the moon. Now it was again a green light on a dock. His count of enchanted objects had diminished by one.

I began to walk about the room, examining various in-definite objects in the half darkness. A large photograph of an elderly man in yachting costume attracted me, hung on the wall over his desk.

"Who's this?"

"That? That's Mr. Dan Cody, old sport."

The name sounded faintly familiar.

"He's dead now. He used to be my best friend years ago."

There was a small picture of Gatsby, also in yachting costume, on the bureau—Gatsby with his head thrown back defiantly—taken apparently when he was about eighteen.

"I adore it!" exclaimed Daisy. "The pompadour! You never told me you had a pompadour—or a yacht."

"Look at this," said Gatsby quickly. "Here's a lot of clippings—about you."

They stood side by side examining it. I was going to ask to see the rubies when the phone rang and Gatsby took up the receiver.

"Yes. . . . Well, I can't talk now. . . . I can't talk now, old sport. . . . I said a *small* town. . . . He must know what a small town is. . . . Well, he's no use to us if Detroit is his idea of a small town. . . . "

He rang off.

"Come here *quick*!" cried Daisy at the window.

The rain was still falling, but the darkness had parted in the west, and there was a pink and golden billow of foamy clouds above the sea.

"Look at that," she whispered, and then after a moment: "I'd like to just get one of those pink clouds and put you in it and push you around."

I tried to go then, but they wouldn't hear of it; perhaps my presence made them feel more satisfactorily alone.

"I know what we'll do," said Gatsby. "We'll have Klip-springer play the piano."

He went out of the room calling "Ewing!" and returned in a few minutes accompanied by an embarrassed, slightly worn young man with shell-rimmed glasses and scanty blonde hair. He was now decently clothed in a "sport-shirt" open at the neck, sneakers and duck trousers of a nebulous hue.

"Did we interrupt your exercises?" inquired Daisy politely.

"I was asleep," cried Mr. Klipspringer, in a spasm of embarrassment. "That is, I'd *been* asleep. Then I got up. . . ."

"Klipspringer plays the piano," said Gatsby, cutting him off. "Don't you, Ewing, old sport?"

"I don't play well. I don't—I hardly play at all. I'm all out of prac——"

"We'll go downstairs," interrupted Gatsby. He flipped a switch. The grey windows disappeared as the house glowed full of light.

In the music room Gatsby turned on a solitary lamp beside the piano. He lit Daisy's cigarette from a trembling match and sat down with her on a couch far across the room where there was no light save what the gleaming floor bounced in from the hall.

When Klipspringer had played "The Love Nest" he turned around on the bench and searched unhappily for Gatsby in the gloom.

"I'm all out of practice, you see. I told you I couldn't play. I'm all out of prac——"

"Don't talk so much, old sport," commanded Gatsby. "Play!"

> *In the morning,*
> *In the evening,*
>   *Ain't we got fun——*

Outside the wind was loud and there was a faint flow of thunder along the Sound. All the lights were going on in West Egg now; the electric trains, men-carrying, were plunging home through the rain from New York. It was the hour of a profound human change and excitement was generating on the air.

> *One thing's sure and nothing's surer*
> *The rich get richer and the poor get—children.*
>   *In the meantime,*
>   *In between time——*

As I went over to say goodbye I saw that the expression of bewilderment had come back into Gatsby's face, as though a faint doubt had occurred to him as to the quality of his present happiness. Almost five years! There must have been moments even that afternoon when Daisy tumbled short of his dreams—not through her own fault but because of the colossal vitality of his illusion. It had gone beyond her, beyond everything. He had thrown himself into it with a creative passion, adding to it all the time, decking it out with every bright feather that drifted his way. No amount of fire or freshness can challenge what a man will store up in his ghostly heart.

As I watched him he adjusted himself a little, visibly. His hand took hold of hers and as she said something low in his ear he turned toward her with a rush of emotion. I think that voice held him most with its fluctuating, feverish warmth because it couldn't be over-dreamed—that voice was a deathless song.

They had forgotten me but Daisy glanced up and held out

her hand; Gatsby didn't know me now at all. I looked once more at them and they looked back at me, remotely, possessed by intense life. Then I went out of the room and down the marble steps into the rain, leaving them there together.

CHAPTER VI

♦

About this time an ambitious young reporter from New York arrived one morning at Gatsby's door and asked him if he had anything to say.

"Anything to say about what?" inquired Gatsby politely.

"Why,—any statement to give out."

It transpired after a confused five minutes that the man had heard Gatsby's name around his office in a connection which he either wouldn't reveal or didn't fully understand. This was his day off and with laudable initiative he had hurried out "to see."

It was a random shot, and yet the reporter's instinct was right. Gatsby's notoriety, spread about by the hundreds who had accepted his hospitality and so become authorities upon his past, had increased all summer until he fell just short of being news. Contemporary legends such as the "underground pipe-line to Canada" attached themselves to him, and there was one persistent story that he didn't live in a house at all, but in a boat that looked like a house and was moved secretly up and down the Long Island shore. Just why these inventions were a source of satisfaction to James

Gatz of North Dakota, isn't easy to say.

James Gatz—that was really, or at least legally, his name.
He had changed it at the age of seventeen and at the specific
moment that witnessed the beginning of his career—when
he saw Dan Cody's yacht drop anchor over the most insidi-
ous flat on Lake Superior. It was James Gatz who had been
loafing along the beach that afternoon in a torn green jersey
and a pair of canvas pants, but it was already Jay Gatsby
who borrowed a row-boat, pulled out to the *Tuolomee* and
informed Cody that a wind might catch him and break him
up in half an hour.

I suppose he'd had the name ready for a long time, even
then. His parents were shiftless and unsuccessful farm people—his imagination had never really accepted them as his
parents at all. The truth was that Jay Gatsby, of West Egg,
Long Island, sprang from his Platonic conception of himself.
He was a son of God—a phrase which, if it means anything,
means just that—and he must be about His Father's Business, the service of a vast, vulgar and meretricious beauty.
So he invented just the sort of Jay Gatsby that a seventeen
year old boy would be likely to invent, and to this conception he was faithful to the end.

For over a year he had been beating his way along the
south shore of Lake Superior as a clam digger and a salmon
fisher or in any other capacity that brought him food and
bed. His brown, hardening body lived naturally through the
half fierce, half lazy work of the bracing days. He knew
women early and since they spoiled him he became contemptuous of them, of young virgins because they were
ignorant, of the others because they were hysterical about

things which in his overwhelming self-absorption he took for granted.

But his heart was in a constant, turbulent riot. The most grotesque and fantastic conceits haunted him in his bed at night. A universe of ineffable gaudiness spun itself out in his brain while the clock ticked on the wash-stand and the moon soaked with wet light his tangled clothes upon the floor. Each night he added to the pattern of his fancies until drowsiness closed down upon some vivid scene with an oblivious embrace. For a while these reveries provided an outlet for his imagination; they were a satisfactory hint of the unreality of reality, a promise that the rock of the world was founded securely on a fairy's wing.

An instinct toward his future glory had led him, some months before, to the small Lutheran college of St. Olaf in southern Minnesota. He stayed there two weeks, dismayed at its ferocious indifference to the drums of his destiny, to destiny itself, and despising the janitor's work with which he was to pay his way through. Then he drifted back to Lake Superior, and he was still searching for something to do on the day that Dan Cody's yacht dropped anchor in the shallows along shore.

Cody was fifty years old then, a product of the Nevada silver fields, of the Yukon, of every rush for metal since Seventy-five. The transactions in Montana copper that made him many times a millionaire found him physically robust but on the verge of softmindedness, and suspecting this an infinite number of women tried to separate him from his money. The none too savory ramifications by which Ella Kaye, the newspaper woman, played Madame de Maintenon to his weakness and sent him to sea in a yacht, were common knowledge to the turgid journalism of 1902. He had been coasting along all too hospitable shores for five years when he turned up as James Gatz's destiny in Little Girl Bay.

To young Gatz, resting on his oars and looking up at the railed deck, that yacht represented all the beauty and glamor in the world. I suppose he smiled at Cody—he had probably discovered that people liked him when he smiled. At any rate Cody asked him a few questions (one of them elicited the brand new name) and found that he was quick, and extravagantly ambitious. A few days later he took him to Duluth and bought him a blue coat, six pair of white duck trousers and a yachting cap. And when the *Tuolomee* left for the West Indies and the Barbary Coast Gatsby left too.

He was employed in a vague personal capacity—while he remained with Cody he was in turn steward, mate, skipper, secretary and even jailor, for Dan Cody sober knew what lavish doings Dan Cody drunk might soon be about and he provided for such contingencies by reposing more and more trust in Gatsby. The arrangement lasted five years during which the boat went three times around the continent. It might have lasted indefinitely except for the fact that Ella Kaye came on board one night in Boston and a week later Dan Cody inhospitably died.

I remember the portrait of him up in Gatsby's bedroom, a grey, florid man with a hard empty face—the pioneer debauchee who during one phase of American life brought back to the eastern seaboard the savage violence of the frontier brothel and saloon. It was indirectly due to Cody that Gatsby drank so little. Sometimes in the course of gay parties women used to rub champagne into his hair; for himself he formed the habit of letting liquor alone.

And it was from Cody that he inherited money—a legacy of twenty-five thousand dollars. He didn't get it. He never understood the legal device that was used against him but what remained of the millions went intact to Ella Kaye. He was left with his singularly appropriate education; the vague contour of Jay Gatsby had filled out to the substantiality of a man.

He told me all this very much later, but I've put it down here with the idea of exploding those first wild rumors about his antecedents, which weren't even faintly true. Moreover he told it to me at a time of confusion, when I had reached the point of believing everything and nothing about him. So I take advantage of this short halt, while Gatsby, so to speak, caught his breath, to clear this set of misconceptions away.

It was a halt, too, in my association with his affairs. For several weeks I didn't see him or hear his voice on the phone—mostly I was in New York, trotting around with Jordan and trying to ingratiate myself with her senile aunt—but finally I went over to his house one Sunday afternoon. I hadn't been there two minutes when somebody brought Tom Buchanan in for a drink. I was startled, naturally, but the really surprising thing was that it hadn't happened before.

They were a party of three on horseback—Tom and a man named Sloane and a pretty woman in a brown riding habit who had been there previously.

"I'm delighted to see you," said Gatsby standing on his porch. "I'm delighted that you dropped in."

As though they cared!

"Sit right down. Have a cigarette or a cigar." He walked around the room quickly, ringing bells. "I'll have something to drink for you in just a minute."

He was profoundly affected by the fact that Tom was there. But he would be uneasy anyhow until he had given them something, realizing in a vague way that that was all they came for. Mr. Sloane wanted nothing. A lemonade? No thanks. A little champagne? Nothing at all, thanks. . . . I'm sorry——

"Did you have a nice ride?"

"Very good roads around here."

"I suppose the automobiles——"

"Yeah."

Moved by an irresistible impulse Gatsby turned to Tom who had accepted the introduction as a stranger.

"I believe we've met somewhere before, Mr. Buchanan."

"Oh, yes," said Tom, gruffly polite but obviously not remembering. "So we did. I remember very well."

"About two weeks ago."

"That 's right. You were with Nick here."

"I know your wife," continued Gatsby, almost aggressively.

"That so?"

Tom turned to me.

"You live near here, Nick?"

"Next door."

"That so?"

Mr. Sloane didn't enter into the conversation but lounged

back haughtily in his chair; the woman said nothing either—until unexpectedly, after two highballs, she became cordial.

"We'll all come over to your next party, Mr. Gatsby," she suggested. "What do you say?"

"Certainly. I'd be delighted to have you."

"Be ver' nice," said Mr. Sloane, without gratitude. "Well—think ought to be starting home."

"Please don't hurry," Gatsby urged them. He had control of himself now and he wanted to see more of Tom. "Why don't you—why don't you stay for supper? I wouldn't be surprised if some other people dropped in from New York."

"You come to supper with *me*," said the lady enthusiastically. "Both of you."

This included me. Mr. Sloane got to his feet.

"Come along," he said—but to her only.

"I mean it," she insisted. "I'd love to have you. Lots of room."

Gatsby looked at me questioningly. He wanted to go and he didn't see that Mr. Sloane had determined he shouldn't.

"I'm afraid I won't be able to," I said.

"Well, you come," she urged, concentrating on Gatsby.

Mr. Sloane murmured something close to her ear.

"We won't be late if we start now," she insisted aloud.

"I haven't got a horse," said Gatsby. "I used to ride in the army but I've never bought a horse. I'll have to follow you in my car. Excuse me for just a minute."

The rest of us walked out on the porch where Sloane and the lady began an impassioned conversation aside.

"My God, I believe the man's coming," said Tom. "Doesn't he know she doesn't want him?"

"She says she does want him."

"She has a big dinner party and he won't know a soul there." He frowned. "I wonder where in the devil he met Daisy. By God, I may be old-fashioned in my ideas but women run around too much these days to suit me. They meet all kinds of crazy fish."

Suddenly Mr. Sloane and the lady walked down the steps and mounted their horses.

"Come on," said Mr. Sloane to Tom. "We're late. We've got to go." And then to me: "Tell him we couldn't wait, will you?"

Tom and I shook hands, the rest of us exchanged a cool nod and they trotted quickly down the drive, disappearing under the August foliage just as Gatsby with hat and light overcoat in hand came out the front door.

Tom was evidently perturbed at Daisy's running around alone, for on the following Saturday night he came with her to Gatsby's party. Perhaps his presence gave the evening its peculiar quality of oppressiveness—it stands out in my memory from Gatsby's other parties that summer. There were the same people, or at least the same sort of people, the same profusion of champagne, the same many-colored, many-keyed commotion, but I felt an unpleasantness in the air, a pervading harshness that hadn't been there before. Or perhaps I had merely grown used to it, grown to accept West Egg as a world complete in itself, with its own standards and its own great figures, second to nothing because it had no consciousness of being so, and now I was looking at it again, through Daisy's eyes. It is invariably saddening to look through new eyes at things upon which you have expended your own powers of adjustment.

They arrived at twilight and as we strolled out among the sparkling hundreds Daisy's voice was playing murmurous tricks in her throat.

"These things excite me *so*," she whispered. "If you want to kiss me any time during the evening, Nick, just let me know and I'll be glad to arrange it for you. Just mention my name. Or present a green card. I'm giving out green——"

"Look around," suggested Gatsby.

"I'm looking around. I'm having a marvelous——"

"You must see the faces of many people you've heard about."

Tom's arrogant eyes roamed the crowd.

"We don't go around very much," he said. "In fact I was just thinking I don't know a soul here."

"Perhaps you know that lady." Gatsby indicated a gorgeous, scarcely human orchid of a woman who sat in state under a white plum tree. Tom and Daisy stared, with that peculiarly unreal feeling that accompanies the recognition of a hitherto ghostly celebrity of the movies.

"She's lovely," said Daisy.

"The man bending over her is her director."

He took them ceremoniously from group to group:

"Mrs. Buchanan . . . and Mr. Buchanan——" After an instant's hesitation he added: "the polo player."

"Oh no," objected Tom quickly. "Not me."

But evidently the sound of it pleased Gatsby for Tom remained "the polo player" for the rest of the evening.

"I've never met so many celebrities!" Daisy exclaimed. "I liked that man—what was his name?—with the sort of blue nose."

Gatsby identified him, adding that he was a small producer.

"Well, I liked him anyhow."

"I'd a little rather not be the polo player," said Tom pleasantly. "I'd rather look at all these famous people in—in oblivion."

Daisy and Gatsby danced. I remember being surprised by his graceful, conservative fox-trot—I had never seen him dance before. Then they sauntered over to my house and sat on the steps for half an hour while at her request I remained watchfully in the garden: "In case there's a fire or a flood," she explained, "or any act of God."

Tom appeared from his oblivion as we were sitting down to supper together. "Do you mind if I eat with some people over here?" he said. "A fellow's getting off some funny stuff."

"Go ahead," answered Daisy genially. "And if you want to take down any addresses here's my little gold pencil. . . ." She looked around after a moment and told me the girl was "common but pretty," and I knew that except for the half hour she'd been alone with Gatsby she wasn't having a good time.

We were at a particularly tipsy table. That was my fault—Gatsby had been called to the phone and I'd enjoyed these same people only two weeks before. But what had amused me then turned septic on the air now.

"How do you feel, Miss Baedeker?"

The girl addressed was trying, unsuccessfully, to slump against my shoulder. At this inquiry she sat up and opened her eyes.

"Wha?"

A massive and lethargic woman, who had been urging Daisy to play golf with her at the local club tomorrow, spoke up in Miss Baedeker's defence:

"Oh she's all right now. When she's had five or six cocktails she always starts screaming like that. I tell her she ought to leave it alone."

"I do leave it alone," affirmed the accused hollowly.

"We heard you yelling, so I said to Doc Civet here: 'There's somebody that needs your help, Doc.' "

"She's much obliged I'm sure," said another friend, without gratitude. "But you got her dress all wet when you stuck her head in the pool."

"Anything I hate is to get my head stuck in a pool," mumbled Miss Baedeker. "They almost drowned me once over in New Jersey."

"Then you ought to leave it alone," countered Doctor Civet.

"Speak for yourself!" cried Miss Baedeker violently. "Your hand shakes. I wouldn't let you operate on me!"

It was like that. Almost the last thing I remember was standing with Daisy and watching the moving picture director and his Star. They were still under the white plum tree and their faces were touching except for a pale thin ray of moonlight between. It occurred to me that he had been very slowly bending toward her all evening to attain this proximity, and even while I watched I saw him stoop one ultimate degree and kiss at her cheek.

"I like her," said Daisy. "I think she's lovely."

But the rest offended her—and inarguably, because it wasn't a gesture but an emotion. She was appalled by West Egg, this unprecedented "place" that Broadway had begotten upon a Long Island fishing village—appalled by its raw vigor that chafed under the old euphemisms and by the too obtrusive fate that herded its inhabitants along a short cut from nothing to nothing. She saw something awful in the very simplicity she failed to understand.

I sat on the front steps with them while they waited for their car. It was dark here in front: only the bright door sent ten square feet of light volleying out into the soft black morning. Sometimes a shadow moved against a dressing-room blind above, gave way to another shadow, an indefinite procession of shadows, who rouged and powdered in an invisible glass.

"Who is this Gatsby anyhow?" demanded Tom suddenly. "Some big bootlegger?"

"Where'd you hear that?" I inquired.

"I didn't hear it. I imagined it. A lot of these newly rich people are just big bootleggers, you know."

"Not Gatsby," I said shortly.

He was silent for a moment. The pebbles of the drive crunched under his feet.

"Well, he certainly must have strained himself to get this menagerie together."

A breeze stirred the grey haze of Daisy's fur collar.

"At least they're more interesting than the people we know," she said with an effort.

"You didn't look so interested."

"Well, I was."

Tom laughed and turned to me.

"Did you notice Daisy's face when that girl asked her to put her under a cold shower?"

Daisy began to sing with the music in a husky, rhythmic

whisper, bringing out a meaning in each word that it had never had before and would never have again. When the melody rose her voice broke up sweetly, following it, in a way contralto voices have, and each change tipped out a little of her warm human magic upon the air.

"Lots of people come who haven't been invited," she said suddenly. "That girl hadn't been invited. They simply force their way in and he's too polite to object."

"I'd like to know who he is and what he does," insisted Tom. "And I think I'll make a point of finding out."

"I can tell you right now," she answered. "He owned some drug stores, a lot of drug stores. He built them up himself."

The dilatory limousine came rolling up the drive.

"Good night, Nick," said Daisy.

Her glance left me and sought the lighted top of the steps where "Three o'Clock in the Morning," a neat sad little waltz of that year, was drifting out the open door. After all, in the very casualness of Gatsby's party there were romantic possibilities totally absent from her world. What was it up there in the song that seemed to be calling her back inside? What would happen now in the dim incalculable hours? Perhaps some unbelievable guest would arrive, a person infinitely rare and to be marvelled at, some authentically radiant young girl who with one fresh glance at Gatsby, one moment of magical encounter, would blot out those five years of unwavering devotion.

I stayed late that night. Gatsby asked me to wait until he was free and I lingered in the garden until the inevitable swimming party had run up, chilled and exalted, from the black beach, until the lights were extinguished in the guest rooms overhead. When he came down the steps at last the tanned skin was drawn unusually tight on his face, and his eyes were bright and tired.

"She didn't like it," he said immediately.

"Of course she did."

"She didn't like it," he insisted. "She didn't have a good time."

He was silent and I guessed at his unutterable depression.

"I feel far away from her," he said. "It's hard to make her understand."

"You mean about the dance?"

"The dance?" He dismissed all the dances he had given with a snap of his fingers. "Old sport, the dance is unimportant."

He wanted nothing less of Daisy than that she should go to Tom and say: "I never loved you." After she had obliterated three years with that sentence they could decide upon the more practical measures to be taken. One of them was that, after she was free, they were to go back to Louisville and be married from her house—just as if it were five years ago.

"And she doesn't understand," he said despairingly. "She used to be able to understand. We'd sit for hours——"

He broke off and began to walk up and down a desolate path of fruit rinds and discarded favors and crushed flowers.

"I wouldn't ask too much of her," I ventured. "You can't repeat the past."

"Can't repeat the past?" he cried incredulously. "Why of course you can!"

He looked around him wildly, as if the past were lurking

here in the shadow of his house, just out of reach of his hand.

"I'm going to fix everything just the way it was before," he said, nodding determinedly. "She'll see."

He talked a lot about the past and I gathered that he wanted to recover something, some idea of himself perhaps, that had gone into loving Daisy. His life had been confused and disordered since then, but if he could once return to a certain starting place and go over it all slowly, he could find out what that thing was. . . .

. . . One autumn night, five years before, they had been walking down the street when the leaves were falling, and they came to a place where there were no trees and the sidewalk was white with moonlight. They stopped here and turned toward each other. Now it was a cool night with that mysterious excitement in it which comes at the two changes of the year. The quiet lights in the houses were humming out into the darkness and there was a stir and bustle among the stars. Out of the corner of his eye Gatsby saw that the blocks of the sidewalk really formed a ladder and mounted to a secret place above the trees—he could climb to it, if he climbed alone, and once there he could suck on the pap of life, gulp down the incomparable milk of wonder.

His heart beat faster and faster as Daisy's white face came up to his own. He knew that when he kissed this girl, and forever wed his unutterable visions to her perishable breath, his mind would never romp again like the mind of God. So he waited, listening for a moment longer to the tuning fork that had been struck upon a star. Then he kissed her. At his lips' touch she blossomed for him like a flower and the incarnation was complete.

Through all he said, even through his appalling sentimentality, I was reminded of something—an elusive rhythm, a fragment of lost words, that I had heard somewhere a long time ago. For a moment a phrase tried to take shape in my mouth and my lips parted like a dumb man's, as though there was more struggling upon them than a wisp of startled air. But they made no sound and what I had almost remembered was uncommunicable forever.

CHAPTER VII

♦

It was when curiosity about Gatsby was at its highest that the lights in his house failed to go on one Saturday night—and, as obscurely as it had begun, his career as Trimalchio was over.

Only gradually did I become aware that the automobiles which turned expectantly into his drive stayed for just a minute and then drove sulkily away. Wondering if he were sick I went over to find out—an unfamiliar butler with a villainous face squinted at me suspiciously from the open door.

"Is Mr. Gatsby sick?"

"Nope." After a pause he added "sir" in a dilatory, grudging way.

"I hadn't seen him around and I was rather worried. Tell him Mr. Carraway came over."

"Who?" he demanded rudely.

"Carraway."

"Carraway. All right, I'll tell him."

Abruptly he slammed the door.

My Finn informed me that Gatsby had dismissed every

servant in his house a week ago and replaced them with half a dozen others who never went into West Egg Village to be bribed by the tradesmen, but ordered moderate supplies over the telephone. The grocery boy reported that the kitchen looked like a pigsty and the general opinion in the village was that the new people weren't servants at all.

Next day Gatsby called me on the phone.

"Going away?" I inquired.

"No, old sport."

"I hear you fired all your servants."

"I wanted somebody who wouldn't gossip. Daisy comes over quite often—in the afternoons."

So the whole caravansary had fallen in like a card house at the disapproval in her eyes.

"They're some people Wolfshiem wanted to do something for. They're all brothers and sisters. They used to run a small hotel."

"I see."

He was calling up at Daisy's request—would I come to lunch at her house tomorrow? Miss Baker would be there. Half an hour later Daisy herself telephoned and seemed relieved to find that I was coming. Something was up. And yet I couldn't believe that they would choose this occasion for a scene—especially for the rather harrowing scene that Gatsby had outlined in the garden.

The next day was broiling, almost the last, certainly the warmest, of the summer. As my train emerged from the tunnel into sunlight, only the hot whistles of the National Biscuit Company broke the simmering hush at noon. The straw seats of the car hovered on the edge of combustion;

the woman next to me perspired delicately for a while into her white shirtwaist and then, as her newspaper dampened under her fingers, lapsed despairingly into deep heat with a desolate cry. Her pocket-book slapped to the floor.

"Oh, my!" she gasped.

I picked it up with a weary bend and handed it back to her holding it at arm's length and by the extreme tip of the corners to indicate that I had no designs upon it—but every one near by, including the woman, suspected me just the same.

"Hot!" said the conductor to familiar faces. "Some weather! . . . Hot! . . . Hot! . . . Hot! . . . Is it hot enough for you? Is it hot? Is it . . . ?"

My commutation ticket came back to me with a dark stain from his hand. That anyone should care in this heat whose flushed lips he kissed, whose head made damp the pajama pocket over his heart!

. . . Through the hall of the Buchanans' house blew a faint wind, carrying the sound of the telephone bell out to Gatsby and me as we waited at the door.

"The master's body!" roared the butler into the mouthpiece. "I'm sorry Madame but we can't furnish it—it's far too hot to touch this noon!"

What he really said was "Yes. . . . Yes. . . . I'll see."

He set down the receiver and came toward us, glistening slightly, to take our stiff straw hats.

"Madame expects you in the salon!" he cried, needlessly indicating the direction. In this heat every extra gesture was an affront to the common store of life.

The room, shadowed well with awnings, was dark and

cool. Daisy and Jordan lay upon an enormous couch, like silver idols, weighing down their own white dresses against the singing breeze of the fans.

"We can't move," they said together.

Jordan's fingers, powdered white over their tan, rested for a moment in mine.

"And Mr. Thomas Buchanan, the athlete?" I inquired.

Simultaneously I heard his voice, gruff, muffled, husky, at the hall telephone.

Gatsby stood in the center of the crimson carpet and gazed around with fascinated eyes. Daisy watched him and laughed her sweet exciting laugh; a tiny gust of powder rose from her bosom into the air.

"The rumor is," whispered Jordan, "that that's Tom's girl on the telephone."

We were silent. The voice in the hall rose high with annoyance. "Very well then, I won't sell you the car at all. . . . I'm under no obligations to you at all. . . . And as for your bothering me about it at lunch time I won't stand that at all!"

"Holding down the receiver," said Daisy cynically.

"No, he's not," I assured her. "It's a bona fide deal. I happen to know about it."

Tom flung open the door, blocked out its space for a moment with his thick body, and hurried into the room.

"Mr. Gatsby!" He put out his broad, flat hand with well-concealed dislike. "I'm glad to see you, sir. . . . Nick. . . ."

"Make us a cold drink," cried Daisy.

As he left the room again she got up and went over to Gatsby, and pulled his face down kissing him on the mouth.

"You know I love you," she murmured.

"You forget there's a lady present," said Jordan.

Daisy looked around doubtfully.

"You kiss Nick too."

"What a low, vulgar girl!"

"I don't care!" cried Daisy and began to clog on the brick fireplace. Then she remembered the heat and sat down guiltily on the couch just as a freshly laundered nurse leading a little girl came into the room.

"Bles-sed pre-cious," she crooned, holding out her arms. "Come to your own mother that loves you."

The child, relinquished by the nurse, rushed across the room and rooted shyly into her mother's dress.

"The Bles-sed pre-cious! Did mother get powder on your old yellowy hair? Stand up now and say How-de-do."

Gatsby and I in turn leaned down and took the small reluctant hand. Afterward he kept looking at the child with surprise. I don't think he had ever really believed in its existence before.

"I got dressed before luncheon," said the child, turning eagerly to Daisy.

"That's because your mother wanted to show you off." Her face bent into the single wrinkle of the small white neck. "You dream, you. You absolute little dream."

"Yes," admitted the child calmly. "Aunt Jordan's got on a white dress too."

"How do you like mother's friends?" Daisy turned her around so that she faced Gatsby. "Do you think they're pretty?"

"Where's Daddy?"

"She doesn't look like her father," explained Daisy. "She

looks like me. She's got my hair and shape of the face."

Daisy sat back upon the couch. The nurse took a step forward and held out her hand.

"Come Pammy."

"Goodbye, sweetheart!"

With a reluctant backward glance the well-disciplined child held to her nurse's hand and was pulled out the door, just as Tom came back, preceding four gin rickeys that clicked full of ice.

Gatsby took up his drink.

"They certainly look cool," he said, with visible tension.

We drank in long greedy swallows.

"I read somewhere that the sun's getting hotter every year," said Tom genially. "It seems that pretty soon the earth's going to fall into the sun—or wait a minute—it's just the opposite—the sun's getting colder every year.

"Come outside," he suggested to Gatsby. "I'd like you to have a look at the place."

I went with them out to the veranda. On the green Sound, stagnant in the heat, one small sail crawled slowly toward the fresher sea. Gatsby's eyes followed it momentarily; he raised his hand and pointed across the bay.

"I'm right across from you."

"So you are."

Our eyes lifted over the rosebeds and the hot lawn and the weedy refuse of the dog days along shore. Slowly the white wings of the boat moved against the blue cool limit of the sky. Ahead lay the scalloped ocean and the abounding blessed isles.

"There's sport for you," said Tom, nodding. "I'd like to be out there with him for about an hour."

We had luncheon in the dining room, darkened, too, against the heat, and drank down nervous gayety with the cold ale.

"What'll we do with ourselves this afternoon," cried Daisy, "and the day after that, and the next thirty years?"

"Don't be morbid," Jordan said. "Life starts all over again when it gets crisp in the fall."

"But it's so hot," insisted Daisy, on the verge of tears. "And everything's so confused. Let's all go to town!"

Her voice struggled on through the heat, beating against it, moulding its senselessness into forms.

"I've heard of making a garage out of a stable," Tom was saying to Gatsby, "but I'm the first man who ever made a stable out of a garage."

"Who wants to go to town?" demanded Daisy insistently. Gatsby's eyes floated toward her. "Ah," she cried, "you look so cool."

Their eyes met, and they stared together at each other, alone in space. With an effort she glanced down at the table.

"You always look so cool," she repeated.

She had told him that she loved him, and Tom Buchanan saw. He was astounded. His mouth opened a little and he looked at Gatsby and then back at Daisy as if he had just recognized her as someone he knew a long time ago.

"You resemble the advertisement of the man," she went on innocently. "You know the advertisement of the man——"

"All right," broke in Tom quickly, "I'm perfectly willing to go to town. Come on—we're all going to town."

He got up, his eyes still flashing between Gatsby and his wife. No one moved.

"Come on!" His temper cracked a little. "What's the matter anyhow? If we're going to town let's start."

His hand, trembling with his effort at self control, bore to his lips the last of his glass of ale. Daisy's voice got us to our feet and out on to the blazing gravel drive.

"Are we just going to go?" she objected. "Like this? Aren't we going to let anyone smoke a cigarette first?"

"Everybody smoked all through lunch."

"Oh, let's have fun," she begged him. "It's too hot to fuss."

He didn't answer.

"Have it your own way," she said. "Come on Jordan."

They went upstairs to get ready while we three men stood there shuffling the hot pebbles with our feet. A silver curve of the moon hovered already in the western sky. Gatsby started to speak, changed his mind, but not before Tom wheeled and faced him expectantly.

"Pardon me?"

"Have you got your stables here?" asked Gatsby with an effort.

"About a quarter of a mile down the road."

"Oh."

A pause.

"I don't see the idea of going to town," broke out Tom savagely. "Women get these notions in their heads——"

"Shall we take anything to drink?" called Daisy from an upper window.

"I'll get some whiskey," answered Tom. He went inside.

Gatsby turned to me rigidly:

"I can't say anything in his house, old sport."

"She's got an indiscreet voice," I remarked. "It's full of——"

I hesitated.

"Her voice is full of money," he said suddenly.

That was it. I'd never understood before. It was full of money—that was the inexhaustible charm that rose and fell in it, the jingle of it, the cymbals' song of it. . . . High in a white palace the king's daughter, the golden girl. . . .

Tom came out of the house wrapping a quart bottle in a towel, followed by Daisy and Jordan wearing small tight hats of metallic cloth and carrying light capes over their arms.

"Shall we all go in my car?" suggested Gatsby. He felt the hot green leather of the seat. "I ought to have left it in the shade."

"Is it standard shift?" demanded Tom.

"Yes."

"Well, you take my coupé and let me drive your car to town."

The suggestion was distasteful to Gatsby.

"I don't think there's much gas," he objected.

"Plenty of gas," said Tom boisterously. He looked at the gauge. "And if it runs out I can stop at a drug store. You can buy anything at a drug store nowadays."

A pause followed this apparently pointless remark. Daisy looked at Tom frowning and an indefinable expression, at once definitely unfamiliar and vaguely recognizable, as if I had only heard it described in words, passed over Gatsby's face.

"Come on, Daisy," said Tom, pressing her with his hand

toward Gatsby's car. "I'll take you in this circus wagon."

He opened the door but she moved out from the circle of his arm.

"You take Nick and Jordan. We'll follow you in the coupé."

She walked close to Gatsby, touching his coat with her hand. Jordan and Tom and I got into the front seat of Gatsby's car, Tom pushed the unfamiliar gears tentatively and we shot off into the oppressive heat leaving them out of sight behind.

"Did you see that?" demanded Tom.

"See what?"

He looked at me keenly, realizing that Jordan and I must have known all along.

"You think I'm pretty dumb, don't you?" he suggested. "Perhaps I am, but I have a—almost a second sight, sometimes, that tells me what to do. Maybe you don't believe that, but science——"

He paused. The immediate contingency overtook him, pulled him back from the edge of the theoretical abyss.

"I've made a small investigation of this fellow," he continued. "I could have gone deeper if I'd known——"

"Do you mean you've been to a medium?" inquired Jordan humorously.

"What?" Confused, he stared at us as we laughed. "A medium?"

"About Gatsby."

"About Gatsby! No, I haven't. I said I'd been making a small investigation of his past."

"And you found he was an Oxford man," said Jordan helpfully.

"An Oxford man!" He was incredulous. "Like hell he is! He wears a pink suit."

"Nevertheless he's an Oxford man."

"Oxford, New Mexico," snorted Tom contemptuously, "or something like that."

"Listen, Tom. If you're such a snob why did you invite him to lunch?" demanded Jordan crossly.

"Daisy invited him; she knew him before we were married—God knows where!"

We were all irritable now with the fading ale and, aware of it, we drove for a while in silence. Then as Doctor T. J. Eckleburg's faded eyes came into sight down the road I remembered Gatsby's caution about gasoline.

"We've got enough to get us to town," said Tom.

"But there's a garage right here," objected Jordan. "I don't want to get stalled in this baking heat."

Tom threw on both brakes impatiently and we slid to an abrupt dusty stop under Wilson's sign. After a moment the proprietor emerged from the interior of his establishment and gazed hollow-eyed at the car.

"Let's have some gas!" cried Tom roughly. "What do you think we stopped for—to admire the view?"

"I'm sick," said Wilson without moving. "I been sick all day."

"What's the matter?"

"I'm all run down."

"Well, shall I help myself?" Tom demanded. "You sounded well enough on the phone."

With an effort Wilson left the shade and support of the doorway and, breathing hard, unscrewed the cap of the tank. In the sunlight his face was green.

"I didn't mean to interrupt your lunch," he said. "But I need money pretty bad and I was wondering what you were going to do with your old car."

"How do you like this one?" inquired Tom. "I bought it last week."

"It's a nice yellow one," said Wilson, as he strained at the handle.

"Like to buy it?"

"Big chance," Wilson smiled faintly. "No, but I could make some money on the other."

"What do you want money for all of a sudden?"

"I've been here too long. I want to get away. My wife and I want to go west."

"Your wife does!" exclaimed Tom, startled.

"She's been talking about it for ten years." He rested for a moment against the pump, shading his eyes. "And now she's going whether she wants to or not. I'm going to get her away."

The coupé flashed by us with a flurry of dust and the flash of a waving hand.

"What do I owe you?" demanded Tom harshly.

"I just got wised up to something funny the last two days," remarked Wilson. "That's why I want to get away. That's why I been bothering you about the car."

"What do I owe you?"

"Dollar twenty."

The relentless beating heat was beginning to confuse me and I had a bad moment there before I realized that so far his suspicions hadn't alighted on Tom. He had discovered that Myrtle had some sort of life apart from him in another world and the shock had made him physically sick. I stared at him and then at Tom, who had made a parallel discovery less than an hour before—and it occurred to me that there was no difference between men, in intelligence or race, so profound as the difference between the sick and the well. Wilson was so sick that he looked guilty, unforgivably guilty—as if he had just got some poor girl with child.

"I'll let you have that car," said Tom. "I'll send it over tomorrow afternoon."

That locality was always vaguely disquieting, even in the broad glare of afternoon, and now I turned my head as though I had been warned of something behind. Over the ashheaps the giant eyes of Doctor T. J. Eckleburg kept their vigil but I perceived, after a moment, that other eyes were regarding us with peculiar intensity from less than twenty feet away.

In one of the windows over the garage the curtains had been moved aside a little and Myrtle Wilson was peering down at the car. So engrossed was she that she had no consciousness of being observed and one emotion after another crept into her face like objects into a slowly developing picture. Her expression was curiously familiar—it was an expression I had often seen on women's faces but on Myrtle Wilson's face it seemed purposeless and inexplicable until I realized that her eyes, wide with jealous terror, were fixed not on Tom but on Jordan Baker, whom she took to be his wife.

There is no confusion like the confusion of a simple mind and as we drove away Tom was feeling the hot whips of panic. His wife and his mistress, until an hour ago secure and inviolate, were slipping precipitately from his control.

Instinct made him step on the accelerator with the double purpose of overtaking Daisy and leaving Wilson behind, and we sped along toward Astoria at fifty miles an hour until, among the spidery girders of the elevated, we came in sight of the easygoing blue coupé.

"Those big movies around Fiftieth Street are cool," suggested Jordan. "I love New York on summer afternoons when everyone's away. There's something very sensuous about it—overripe, as if all sorts of funny fruits were going to fall into your hands."

The word "sensuous" had the effect of further disquieting Tom but before he could invent a protest the coupé came to a stop and Daisy signalled us to draw up alongside.

"Where are we going?" she cried.

"How about the movies?"

"It's so hot," she complained. "You go. We'll ride around and meet you after." With an effort her wit rose faintly, "We'll meet you on some corner. I'll be the man smoking two cigarettes."

"We can't argue about it here," Tom said impatiently, as a truck gave out a cursing whistle behind us. "You follow me to the south side of Central Park, in front of the Plaza."

Several times he turned his head and looked back for their car, and if the traffic delayed them he slowed up until they came into sight. I think he was afraid they would dart down a side street and out of his life forever.

But they didn't. And we all took the less explicable step of engaging the parlor of a suite in the Plaza Hotel.

The prolonged and tumultuous argument that ended by herding us into that room eludes me, though I have a sharp physical memory that, in the course of it, my underwear kept climbing like a damp snake around my legs and inter-mittent beads of sweat raced cool across my back. The notion originated with Daisy's suggestion that we hire five bathrooms and take cold baths, and then assumed more tangible form as "a place to have a mint julep." Each of us said over and over that it was a "crazy idea"—we all talked at once to a baffled clerk and thought, or pretended to think, that we were being very funny. . . .

The room was large and stifling, and, though it was already four o'clock, opening the windows admitted only a gust of hot shrubbery from the Park. Daisy went to the mirror and stood with her back to us fixing her hair.

"It's a swell suite," whispered Jordan respectfully and everyone laughed.

"Open another window," commanded Daisy, without turning around.

"There aren't any more."

"Well, we'd better telephone for an axe——"

"The thing to do is to forget about the heat," said Tom impatiently. "You make it ten times worse by crabbing about it."

He unrolled the bottle of whiskey from the towel and put it on the table.

"Why not let her alone, old sport," remarked Gatsby. "You're the one that wanted to come to town."

There was a moment of silence. The telephone book slipped from its nail and splashed to the floor, whereupon Jordan whispered "Excuse me"—but this time no one laughed.

"I'll pick it up," I offered.

"I've got it." Gatsby examined the parted string, muttered "Hum!" in an interested way, and tossed the book on a chair.

"That's a great expression of yours, isn't it?" said Tom sharply.

"What is?"

"All this 'old sport' business. Where'd you pick that up?"

"Now see here, Tom," said Daisy, turning around from the mirror, "if you're going to make personal remarks I won't stay here a minute. Call up and order some ice for the mint julep."

As Tom took up the receiver the compressed heat exploded into sound and we were listening to the portentous chords of Mendelssohn's Wedding March from the ballroom below.

"Imagine marrying anybody in this heat!" cried Jordan dismally.

"Still—I was married in the middle of June," Daisy remembered. "Louisville in June! Somebody fainted. Who was it fainted, Tom?"

"Biloxi," he answered shortly.

"A man named Biloxi. 'Blocks' Biloxi, and he made boxes—that's a fact—and he was from Biloxi, Tennessee."

"They carried him into my house," appended Jordan, "because we lived just two doors from the church. And he stayed three weeks, until Daddy told him he had to get out. The day after he left Daddy died." After a moment she added as if she might have sounded irreverent, "There wasn't any connection."

"I used to know a Bill Biloxi from Memphis," I remarked.

"That was his cousin. I knew his whole family history

before he left. He gave me an aluminum putter that I use today."

The music had died down as the ceremony began and now a long cheer floated in at the window, followed by intermittent cries of "Yea—ea—ea!" and finally by a burst of jazz as the dancing began.

"We're getting old," said Daisy. "If we were young we'd rise and dance."

"Remember Biloxi," Jordan warned her. "Where'd you know him, Tom?"

"Biloxi?" He concentrated with an effort. "I didn't know him. He was a friend of Daisy's."

"He was not," she denied. "I'd never seen him before. He came down in the private car."

"Well, he said he knew you. He said he was raised in Louisville. Asa Bird brought him around at the last minute and asked if we had room for him."

Jordan smiled.

"He was probably bumming his way home. He told me he was president of your class at Yale."

Tom and I looked at each other blankly.

"Biloxi?"

"First place we didn't have any president——"

Gatsby's foot beat a short restless tattoo and Tom eyed him suddenly.

"By the way, Mr. Gatsby, I understand you're an Oxford man."

"Not exactly."

"Oh, yes, I understand you went to Oxford."

"Yes—I went there."

A pause. Then Tom's voice, incredulous and insulting:

"You must have gone there about the time Biloxi went to New Haven."

Another pause. A waiter knocked and came in with crushed mint and ice but the silence was unbroken by his "Thank you" and the soft closing of the door. This tremendous detail was to be cleared up at last.

"I told you I went there," said Gatsby.

"I heard you, but I'd like to know when."

"It was in nineteen-nineteen. I only stayed five months. That's why I can't really call myself an Oxford man."

Tom glanced around to see if we mirrored his unbelief. But we were all looking at Gatsby.

"It was an opportunity they gave to some of the officers after the Armistice," he continued. "We could go to any of the universities in England or France."

I wanted to get up and slap him on the back. I had one of those renewals of complete faith in him that I'd experienced before.

Daisy rose, smiling faintly, and went to the table.

"Open the whiskey, Tom," she ordered. "And I'll make you a mint julep. Then you won't seem so stupid to yourself . . . . Look at the mint!"

"Wait a minute," snapped Tom. "I want to ask Mr. Gatsby one more question."

"Go on," Gatsby said politely.

"What kind of a row are you trying to cause in my house anyhow?"

They were out in the open at last and Gatsby was content.

"He isn't causing a row." Daisy looked desperately from one to the other. "You're causing a row. Please have a little self control."

"Self control!" repeated Tom incredulously. "I suppose the latest thing is to sit back and let Mr. Nobody from Nowhere make love to your wife. Well, if that's the idea you can count me out. . . . Nowadays people begin by sneering at family life and family institutions and next they'll throw everything overboard and have intermarriage between black and white."

Flushed with his impassioned gibberish he saw himself standing alone on the last barrier of civilization.

"We're all white here," murmured Jordan.

"I know I'm not very popular. I don't give big parties. I suppose you've got to make your house into a pigsty in order to have any friends—in the modern world."

Angry as I was, as we all were, I was tempted to laugh whenever he opened his mouth. The transition from libertine to prig was so complete.

"I've got something to tell *you,* old sport,—" began Gatsby. But Daisy guessed at his intention.

"Please don't!" she interrupted helplessly. "Please let's all go home. Why don't we all go home?"

"That's a good idea." I got up. "Come on, Tom. Nobody wants a drink."

"I want to know what Mr. Gatsby has to tell me."

"Your wife doesn't love you," said Gatsby quietly. "She's never loved you. She loves me."

"You must be crazy!" exclaimed Tom automatically.

Gatsby sprang to his feet, vivid with excitement.

"She never loved you, do you hear?" he cried. "She only married you because I was poor and she was tired of waiting for me. It was a terrible mistake, but in her heart she never loved anyone except me!"

At this point Jordan and I tried to go but Tom and Gatsby insisted with competitive firmness that we remain— as though neither of them had anything to conceal and it would be a privilege to partake vicariously of their emotions.

"Sit down Daisy." Tom's voice groped unsuccessfully for the paternal note. "What's been going on? I want to hear all about it."

"I told you what's been going on," said Gatsby. "Going on for five years—and you didn't know."

Tom turned to Daisy sharply.

"You've been seeing this fellow for five years?"

"Not seeing," said Gatsby. "No, we couldn't meet. But both of us loved each other all that time, old sport, and you didn't know. I used to laugh sometimes—" but there was no laughter in his eyes, "to think that you didn't know."

"Oh—that's all." Tom tapped his thick fingers together like a clergyman and leaned back in his chair.

"You're crazy!" he exploded. "I can't speak about what happened five years ago because I didn't know Daisy then— and I'll be damned if I see how you got within a mile of her unless you brought the groceries to the back door. But all the rest of that's a God Damned lie. Daisy loved me when she married me and she loves me now."

"No," said Gatsby, shaking his head.

"She does, though. The trouble is that sometimes she gets foolish ideas in her head and doesn't know what she's doing." He nodded sagely. "And what's more, I love Daisy too. Once in a while I go off on a spree and make a fool of myself, but I always come back, and in my heart I love her all the time."

"You're revolting," said Daisy. She turned to me and her voice, dropping an octave lower, filled the room with thrilling scorn: "Do you know why we left Chicago? I'm surprised that they didn't treat you to the story of that little spree."

Gatsby walked over and stood beside her.

"Daisy, that's all over now," he said earnestly. "It doesn't matter any more. Just tell him the truth—that you never loved him—and it's all wiped out forever."

She looked at him blindly. "Why,—how could I love him—possibly?"

"You never loved him."

She hesitated. Her eyes fell on Jordan and me with a sort of appeal, as though she realized at last what she was doing—and as though she had never, all along, intended doing anything at all. But it was done now. It was too late.

"I never loved him," she said, with perceptible reluctance.

"Not at Kapiolani?" demanded Tom suddenly.

"No."

From the ballroom beneath, muffled and suffocating chords were drifting up on hot waves of air.

"Not that day I carried you down from the Punch Bowl to keep your shoes dry?" There was a husky tenderness in his tone. " . . . Daisy?"

"Please don't." Her voice was cold but the rancour was gone from it. She looked at Gatsby. "There, Jay," she said—but her hand as she tried to light a cigarette was trembling. Suddenly she threw the cigarette and the burning match on the carpet.

"Oh, you want too much!" she cried to Gatsby. "I love

you now—isn't that enough? I can't help what's past." She began to sob helplessly. "I did love him once—but I loved you too."

Gatsby's eyes opened and closed.

"You loved me *too*?" he repeated.

"Even that's a lie," said Tom savagely. "She didn't know you were alive. Why,—there're things between Daisy and me that you'll never know, things that neither of us can ever forget."

The words seemed to bite physically into Gatsby.

"I want to speak to Daisy alone," he insisted. "She's all excited now——"

"Even alone I can't say I never loved Tom," she admitted in a pitiful voice. "It wouldn't be true."

"Of course it wouldn't," agreed Tom.

She turned to her husband.

"As if it mattered to you," she said.

"Of course it matters. I'm going to take better care of you from now on."

"You don't understand," said Gatsby, with a touch of panic. "You're not going to take care of her any more."

"I'm not?" Tom opened his eyes wide and laughed. He could afford to control himself now. "Why's that?"

"Daisy's leaving you."

"Nonsense."

"I am, though," she said with a visible effort.

"She's not leaving me!" Tom's words suddenly leaned down over Gatsby. "Certainly not for a common swindler who'd have to steal the ring he put on her finger."

"I won't stand this!" cried Daisy. "Oh, please let's get out."

"Who are you anyhow?" broke out Tom. "You're one of that bunch that hangs around with Meyer Wolfshiem—that much I happen to know. I've made a little investigation into your affairs—and I'll carry it further tomorrow."

"You can suit yourself about that, old sport," said Gatsby steadily.

"I found out what your 'drug stores' were." He turned to us and spoke rapidly. "He and this Wolfshiem bought up a lot of side-street drug stores here and in Chicago and sold grain alcohol over the counter. That's one of his little stunts. I picked him for a bootlegger the first time I saw him and I wasn't far wrong."

"What about it?" said Gatsby politely. "I guess your friend Walter Chase wasn't too proud to come in on it."

"And you left him in the lurch, didn't you? You let him go to jail for a month over in New Jersey. God! You ought to hear Walter on the subject of *you*."

"He came to us dead broke. He was very glad to pick up some money, old sport."

"Don't you call me 'old sport'!" cried Tom. Gatsby said nothing. "Walter could have you up on the betting laws too, but Wolfshiem scared him into shutting his mouth."

That unfamiliar yet recognizable look was back again in Gatsby's face.

"That drug store business was just small change," continued Tom slowly, "but you've got something on now that Walter's afraid to tell me about."

I glanced at Daisy who was staring terrified between Gatsby and her husband and at Jordan who had begun to balance an invisible but absorbing object on the tip of her chin. Then I turned back to Gatsby—and was startled at his expression. He looked—and this is said in all contempt for the babbled slander of his garden—as if he had "killed a man." For a moment the set of his face could be described in just that fantastic way.

It passed, and he began to talk excitedly to Daisy, denying everything, defending his name against accusations that had not been made. But with every word she was drawing further and further into herself, so he gave that up and only the dead dream fought on as the afternoon slipped away, trying to touch what was no longer tangible, struggling unhappily, undespairingly, toward that lost voice across the room.

The voice begged again to go.

"*Please,* Tom! I can't stand this any more."

Her frightened eyes told that whatever intentions, whatever courage she had had, were definitely gone.

"You two start on home, Daisy," said Tom. "In Mr. Gatsby's car."

She looked at Tom, alarmed now, but he insisted with magnanimous scorn.

"Go on. He won't annoy you. I think he realizes that his presumptuous little flirtation is over."

They were gone, without a word, snapped out, made accidental, isolated like ghosts even from our pity.

After a moment Tom got up and began wrapping the unopened bottle of whiskey in the towel.

"Want any of this stuff? Jordan? . . . Nick?"

I didn't answer.

"Nick?" He asked again.

"What?"

"Want any?"

"No . . . I just remembered that today's my birthday."

I was thirty. Before me stretched the portentous menacing road of a new decade.

It was seven o'clock when we got into the coupé with him and started for Long Island. Tom talked incessantly, exulting and laughing, but his voice was as remote from Jordan and me as the foreign clamor on the sidewalk or the tumult of the elevated overhead. Human sympathy has its limits and we were content to let all their tragic arguments fade with the city lights behind. Thirty—the promise of a decade of loneliness, a thinning list of single men to know, a thinning brief-case of enthusiasm, thinning hair. But there was Jordan beside me who, unlike Daisy, was too wise ever to carry well-forgotten dreams from age to age. As we passed over the dark bridge her wan face fell lazily against my coat's shoulder and the formidable stroke of thirty died away with the reassuring pressure of her hand.

So we drove on toward death through the cooling twilight.

The young Greek, Michaelis, who ran the coffee joint beside the ashheaps was the principal witness at the inquest. He had slept through the heat, until after five, when he strolled over to the garage and found George Wilson sick in his office—really sick, pale as his own pale hair and shaking all over. Michaelis advised him to go to bed but Wilson refused, saying that he'd miss a lot of business if he did. While his neighbor was trying to persuade him a violent racket broke out overhead.

"I've got my wife locked in up there," explained Wilson calmly. "She's going to stay there till the day after tomorrow and then we're going to move away."

Michaelis was astonished; they had been neighbors for four years and Wilson had never seemed faintly capable of such a statement. Generally he was one of these worn-out men: when he wasn't working he sat on a chair in the doorway and stared at the people and the cars that passed along the road. When anyone spoke to him he invariably laughed in an agreeable colorless way. He was his wife's man and not his own.

So naturally Michaelis tried to find out what had happened, but Wilson wouldn't say a word—instead he began to throw curious, suspicious glances at his visitor and ask him what he'd been doing at certain times on certain days. Just as the latter was getting uneasy some workmen came past the door bound for his restaurant and Michaelis took the opportunity to get away, intending to come back later. But he didn't. He supposed he forgot to, that's all. When he came outside again a little after seven he was reminded of the conversation because he heard Mrs. Wilson's voice, loud and scolding, downstairs in the garage.

"Beat me!" he heard her cry. "Throw me down and beat me, you dirty little coward!"

A moment later she rushed out into the dusk, waving her hands and shouting; before he could move from his door the business was over.

The "death car," as the newspapers called it, didn't stop; it came out of the gathering darkness, wavered tragically for a moment and then disappeared around the next bend. Michaelis wasn't even sure of its color—he told the first policeman that it was light green. The other car, the one going toward New York, came to rest a hundred yards beyond, and its driver hurried back to where Myrtle Wilson, her life violently extinguished, knelt in the road and mingled her thick, dark blood with the dust.

Michaelis and this man reached her first but when they had torn open her shirtwaist still damp with perspiration they saw that her left breast was swinging loose like a flap and there was no need to listen for the heart beneath. The mouth was wide open and ripped at the corners as though she had choked a little in giving up the tremendous vitality she had stored so long.

We saw the three or four automobiles and the crowd when we were still some distance away.

"Wreck!" said Tom. "That's good. Wilson'll have a little business at last."

He slowed down, but still without any intention of stopping until, as we came nearer, the hushed intent faces of the people at the garage door made him automatically put on the brakes.

"We'll take a look," he said doubtfully, "just a look."

I became aware now of a hollow, wailing sound which issued incessantly from the garage, a sound which as we got out of the coupé and walked toward the door resolved itself into the words "Oh My God!" uttered over and over in a gasping moan.

"There's some bad trouble here," said Tom excitedly.

He reached up on tiptoes and peered over a circle of heads into the garage which was lit only by a yellow light in a swinging wire basket overhead. Then he made a harsh sound in his throat and with a violent, thrusting movement of his powerful arms pushed his way through.

The circle closed up again with a running murmur of

expostulation; it was a minute before I could see anything at all. Then new arrivals disarranged the line and Jordan and I were pushed suddenly inside.

Myrtle Wilson's body wrapped in a blanket and then in another blanket as though she suffered from a chill in the hot night lay on a work table by the wall and Tom, with his back to us, was bending over it, motionless. Next to him stood a motor cycle policeman taking down names with much sweat and correction in a little book. At first I couldn't find the source of the high, groaning words that echoed clamorously through the bare garage—then I saw Wilson standing on the raised threshold of his office, swaying back and forth and holding to the doorposts with both hands. Some man was talking to him in a low voice and attempting from time to time to lay a hand on his shoulder, but Wilson neither heard nor saw. His eyes would drop slowly from the swinging light to the laden table by the wall and then jerk back to the light again and he gave out incessantly his high horrible call.

"O my Ga-od! O my Ga-od! O Ga-od! O my Ga-od!"

Presently Tom lifted his head with a jerk and after staring around the garage with glazed eyes addressed a mumbled incoherent remark to the policeman.

"M-a-v—" the policeman was saying, "—o———"

"No, —r—" corrected the man, "M-a-v-r-o———"

"Listen to me!" muttered Tom fiercely.

"r—" said the policeman, "o———"

"g———"

"g—" He looked up as Tom's broad hand fell sharply on his shoulder. "What you want, fella?"

"What happened—that's what I want to know!"

"Auto hit her. Ins'antly killed."

"Instantly killed," repeated Tom, staring.

"She ran out ina road. Son-of-a-bitch didn't even stopus car."

"There was two cars," said Michaelis. "One comin', one goin', see?"

"Going where?" asked the policeman keenly.

"One goin' each way. Well, she—" His hand rose toward the blankets but stopped half way and fell to his side, "—she ran out there an' the one comin' from N'York knock right into her goin' thirty or forty miles an hour."

"What's the name of this place here?" demanded the officer.

"Hasn't got any name."

A pale, well dressed Negro stepped near.

"It was a yellow car," he said. "Big yellow car. New."

"See the accident?" asked the policeman.

"No, but the car passed me down the road, going faster'n forty. Going fifty, sixty."

"Come here and let's have your name. Look out now. I want to get his name."

Some words of this conversation must have reached Wilson swaying in the office door for suddenly a new theme found voice among his gasping cries.

"You don't have to tell me what kind of car it was! I know what kind of car it was!"

Watching Tom I saw the wad of muscle back of his shoulder tighten under his coat. He walked quickly over to Wilson and standing in front of him seized him firmly by the upper arms.

"You've got to pull yourself together," he said with soothing gruffness.

Wilson's eyes fell upon Tom; he started up on his tiptoes and then would have collapsed to his knees had not Tom held him upright.

"Listen," said Tom, shaking him a little. "I just got here a minute ago, from New York. I was bringing you that coupé we've been talking about. That yellow car I was driving this afternoon wasn't mine, do you hear? I haven't seen it all afternoon."

Only the Negro and I were near enough to hear what he said but the policeman caught something in the tone and looked over with truculent eyes.

"What's all that?" he demanded.

"I'm a friend of his." Tom turned his head but kept his hands firm on Wilson's body. "He says he knows the car that did it. . . . It was a yellow car."

Some dim impulse moved the policeman to look suspiciously at Tom.

"And what color's your car?"

"It's a blue car, a coupé."

"We've come straight from New York," I said.

Someone who had been driving a little behind us confirmed this and the policeman turned away.

"Now if you'll let me have that name again correct——"

Picking up Wilson like a doll Tom carried him into the office, set him down in a chair and came back.

"If somebody'll come here and sit with him!" he snapped authoritatively. He watched while the two men standing closest glanced at each other and went unwillingly into the room. Then Tom shut the door on them and came down the single step, his eyes avoiding the table. As he passed close to me he whispered "Let's get out."

Self consciously, with his authoritative arms breaking the way, we pushed through the still gathering crowd, passing a hurried doctor, case in hand, who had been sent for in wild hope half an hour ago.

Tom drove slowly until we were beyond the bend—then his foot came down hard and the coupé raced along through the night. In a little while I heard a low husky sob and saw that the tears were overflowing down his face.

"The God Damn coward!" he whimpered. "He didn't even stop his car."

The Buchanans' house floated suddenly toward us through the dark, rustling trees. Tom stopped beside the porch and looked up at the second floor where two windows bloomed with light among the vines.

"Daisy's home," he said. As we got out of the car he glanced at me and frowned slightly.

"I ought to have dropped you in West Egg, Nick. There's nothing we can do tonight."

A change had come over him and he spoke gravely, and with decision. As we walked across the moonlit gravel to the porch he disposed of the situation in a few brisk phrases.

"I'll telephone for a taxi to take you home, and while you're waiting you and Jordan better go in the kitchen and have them get you some supper—if you want any." He opened the door. "Come in."

"No thanks. But I'd be glad if you'd order me the taxi. I'll wait outside."

Jordan put her hand on my arm.

"Won't you come in, Nick?"

"No thanks."

I was feeling a little sick and I wanted to be alone. But Jordan lingered for a moment more.

"It's only half past nine," she said.

I'd be damned if I'd go in; I'd had enough of all of them for one day and suddenly that included Jordan too. She must have seen something of this in my expression for she turned abruptly away and ran up the porch steps into the house. I sat down for a few minutes with my head in my hands, until I heard the phone taken up inside and the butler's voice calling a taxi. Then I walked slowly down the drive away from the house intending to wait by the gate.

I hadn't gone twenty yards when I heard my name and Gatsby stepped from between two bushes into the path. I must have felt pretty weird by that time because I could think of nothing except the luminosity of his pink suit under the moon.

"What are you doing?" I inquired.

"Just standing here, old sport."

Somehow that seemed a despicable occupation. For all I knew he was going to rob the house in a moment; I wouldn't have been surprised to see sinister faces, the faces of "Wolfshiem's people," behind him in the dark shrubbery.

"Did you see any trouble on the road?" he asked after a minute.

"Yes."

He hesitated.

"Was she killed?"

"Yes."

"I thought so; I told Daisy I thought so. It's better that the shock should all come at once. She stood it pretty well."

He spoke as if Daisy's reaction was the only thing that mattered.

"I got to West Egg by a side road," he went on, "and left the car in my garage. I don't think anybody saw us but of course I can't be sure."

I disliked him so much by this time that I didn't find it necessary to tell him he was wrong.

"Who was the woman?" he inquired.

"Her name was Wilson. Her husband owns the garage. How the devil did it happen?"

"Well, I tried to swing the wheel——" He broke off, and suddenly I guessed at the truth.

"Was Daisy driving?"

"Yes," he said after a moment, "but of course I'll say I was. You see, when we left New York she was very nervous and she thought it would steady her to drive—and this woman rushed out at us just as we were passing a car coming the other way. It all happened in a minute but it seemed to me that she wanted to speak to us, thought we were somebody she knew. Well, first Daisy turned away from the woman toward the other car, and then she lost her nerve and turned back. The second my hand reached the wheel I felt the shock—it must have killed her instantly."

"It ripped her open——"

"Don't tell me, old sport." He winced. "Anyhow—Daisy stepped on it. I tried to make her stop but she couldn't so I pulled on the emergency brake. Then she fell over into my lap and I drove on.

"She'll be all right tomorrow," he said presently. "I'm just going to wait here and see if he tries to bother her about that unpleasantness this afternoon. She's locked herself into her room and if he tries any brutality she's going to turn the light out and on again."

"He won't touch her," I said. "He's not thinking about her."

"I don't trust him, old sport."

"How long are you going to wait?"

"All night if necessary. Anyhow till they all go to bed."

A new point of view occurred to me. Suppose Tom found out that Daisy had been driving. He might think he saw a connection in it—he might think anything. I looked at the house: there were two or three bright windows downstairs and the pink glow from Daisy's room on the second floor.

"You wait here," I said. "I'll see if there's any sign of a commotion."

I walked back along the border of the lawn, traversed the gravel softly and tiptoed up the veranda steps. The drawing room curtains were open and I saw that the room was empty. Crossing the porch where we had dined that June night three months before I came to a small rectangle of light which I guessed was the pantry window. The blind was drawn but I found a rift at the sill.

Daisy and Tom were sitting opposite each other at the kitchen table with a plate of cold fried chicken between them and two bottles of ale. He was talking intently across the table at her and in his earnestness his hand had fallen upon and covered her own. Once in a while she looked up at him and nodded in agreement.

They weren't happy, and neither of them had touched the chicken or the ale—and yet they weren't unhappy either. There was an unmistakable air of natural intimacy about the picture and anybody would have said that they were conspiring together.

As I tiptoed from the porch I heard my taxi feeling its way along the dark road toward the house. Gatsby was waiting where I had left him in the drive.

"Is it all quiet up there?" he asked anxiously.

"Yes, it's all quiet." I hesitated. "You'd better come home and get some sleep."

He shook his head.

"I want to wait here till Daisy goes to bed. Good night, old sport."

He put his hands in his coat pockets and turned back eagerly to his scrutiny of the house, as though my presence marred the sacredness of the vigil. So I walked away and left him standing there in the moonlight—watching over nothing.

CHAPTER VIII

♦

I couldn't sleep all night; a fog-horn was groaning incessantly on the Sound, and I tossed half sick between grotesque reality and savage frightening dreams. Toward dawn I heard a taxi go up Gatsby's drive and immediately I jumped out of bed and began to dress—I felt that I had something to tell him, something to warn him about and morning would be too late.

Crossing his lawn I saw that his front door was still open and he was leaning against a table in the hall, heavy with dejection or sleep.

"Nothing happened," he said wanly. "I waited, and about four o'clock she came to the window and stood there for a minute and then turned out the light."

His house had never seemed so enormous to me as it did that night when we hunted through the great rooms for cigarettes. We pushed aside curtains that were like pavilions and felt over innumerable feet of dark wall for electric light switches—once I tumbled with a sort of splash upon the keys of a ghostly piano. There was an inexplicable amount of dust everywhere and the rooms were musty as though they hadn't been aired for many days. I found the humidor on an unfamiliar table with two stale dry cigarettes inside. Throwing open the French windows of the drawing room we sat smoking out into the darkness.

"You ought to go away," I said. "It's pretty certain they'll trace your car."

"Go away *now*, old sport?"

"Go to Atlantic City for a week, or up to Montreal."

He wouldn't consider it. He couldn't possibly leave Daisy until he knew what she was going to do. He was clutching at some last hope and I couldn't bear to shake him free.

It was this night that he told me the strange story of his youth with Dan Cody—told it to me because "Jay Gatsby" had broken up like glass against Tom's hard malice and the long secret extravaganza was played out. I think that he would have acknowledged anything, now, without reserve, but he wanted to talk about Daisy.

She was the first "nice" girl he had ever known. In various unrevealed capacities he had come in contact with such people but always with indiscernible barbed wire between. He found her excitingly desirable. He went to her house, at first with other officers from Camp Taylor, then alone. It amazed him—he had never been in such a beautiful house before. But what gave it an air of breathless intensity was that Daisy lived there—it was as casual a thing to her as his tent out at camp was to him. There was a ripe mystery about it, a hint of bedrooms upstairs more beautiful and cool than other bedrooms, of gay and radiant activities taking place through its corridors and of romances that were not musty and laid away already in lavender but fresh and breathing and redolent of this year's shining motor cars and of dances whose flowers were scarcely withered. It excited him too that many men had already loved Daisy—it increased her value in his eyes. He felt their presence all about the house, pervading the air with the shades and echoes of still vibrant emotions.

But he knew that he was in Daisy's house by a colossal accident. However glorious might be his future as Jay Gatsby, he was at present a penniless young man without a past, and at any moment the invisible cloak of his uniform might slip from his shoulders. So he made the most of his time. He took what he could get, ravenously and unscrupulously—eventually he took Daisy one still October night, took her because he had no real right to touch her hand.

He might have despised himself, for he had certainly taken her under false pretenses. I don't mean that he had traded on his phantom millions, but he had deliberately given Daisy a sense of security; he let her believe that he was a person from much the same strata as herself—that he was fully able to take care of her. As a matter of fact he had no such facilities—he had no comfortable family standing behind him and he was liable at the whim of an impersonal government to be blown anywhere about the world.

But he didn't despise himself and it didn't turn out as he had imagined. He had intended, probably, to take what he could and go—but now he found that he had committed himself to the following of a grail. He knew that Daisy was extraordinary but he didn't realize just how extraordinary a "nice" girl could be. She vanished into her rich house, into her rich, full life, leaving Gatsby—nothing. He felt married to her, that was all.

When they met again two days later it was Gatsby who was breathless, who was somehow betrayed. Her porch was bright with the bought luxury of star-shine; the wicker of the settee squeaked fashionably as she turned toward him and he kissed her curious and lovely mouth. She had caught a cold and it made her voice huskier and more charming than ever and Gatsby was overwhelmingly aware of the youth and mystery that wealth imprisons and preserves, of the freshness of many clothes and of Daisy, gleaming like silver, safe and proud above the hot struggles of the poor.

"I can't describe to you how surprised I was to find out I loved her, old sport. I even hoped for a while that she'd throw me over, but she didn't, because she was in love with me too. She thought I knew a lot because I knew different things from her. . . . Well, there I was, way off my ambitions, getting deeper in love every minute, and all of a sudden I didn't care. What was the use of doing great things if I could have a better time telling her what I was going to do?"

On the last afternoon before he went abroad he sat with Daisy in his arms for a long, silent time. It was a cold fall day with fire in the room and her cheeks flushed. Now and then she moved and he changed his arm a little and once he kissed her dark shining hair. The afternoon had made them tranquil for a while as if to give them a deep memory for the long parting the next day promised. They had never been

closer in their month of love nor communicated more profoundly one with another, than when she brushed silent lips
against his coat's shoulder or when he touched the end of
her fingers, gently, as though she were asleep.

He did extraordinarily well in the war. He was a captain
before he went to the front and following the Argonne
battles he got his majority and the command of the divi-
sional machine guns. After the Armistice he tried frantically
to get home but some complication or misunderstanding
sent him to Oxford instead. He was worried now—there
was a quality of nervous despair in Daisy's letters. She
didn't see why he couldn't come. She was feeling the pressure of the world outside and she wanted to see him and feel
his presence beside her and be reassured that she was doing
the right thing after all.

For Daisy was young and her artificial world was redolent of orchids and pleasant, cheerful snobbery and orches-
tras which set the rhythm of the year, summing up the
sadness and suggestiveness of life in new tunes. All night the
saxophones wailed the hopeless comment of the "Beale
Street Blues" while a hundred pairs of golden and silver
slippers shuffled the shining dust. At the grey tea hour there
were always rooms that throbbed incessantly with this low
sweet fever, while fresh faces drifted here and there like rose
petals blown by the sad horns around the floor.

Through this twilight universe Daisy began to move
again with the season; suddenly she was again keeping half
a dozen dates a day with half a dozen men and drowsing
asleep at dawn with the beads and chiffon of an evening

dress tangled among dying orchids on the floor beside her bed. And all the time something within her was crying for a decision. She wanted her life shaped now, immediately—and the decision must be made by some force—of love, of money, of unquestionable practicality—that was close at hand.

That force took shape in the middle of spring with the arrival of Tom Buchanan. There was a wholesome bulkiness about his person and his position and Daisy was flattered. Doubtless there was a certain struggle and a certain relief. The letter reached Gatsby while he was still at Oxford.

It was dawn now on Long Island and we went about opening the rest of the windows downstairs, filling the house with grey turning, gold turning light. The shadow of a tree fell abruptly across the dew and ghostly birds began to sing among the blue leaves. There was a slow pleasant movement in the air, scarcely a wind, promising a cool lovely day.

"I don't think she ever loved him." Gatsby turned around from a window and looked at me challengingly. "You must remember, old sport, she was very excited this afternoon. He told her those things in a way that frightened her—that made it look as if I was some kind of cheap sharper. And the result was she hardly knew what she was saying."

He sat down gloomily.

"Of course she might have loved him, just for a minute, when they were first married—and loved me more even then, do you see?"

Suddenly he came out with a curious remark:

"In any case," he said, "it was just personal."

What could you make of that, except to suspect some intensity in his conception of the affair that couldn't be measured?

He came back from France when Tom and Daisy were still on their wedding trip, and made a miserable but irresistible journey to Louisville on the last of his army pay. He stayed there a week, walking the streets where their footsteps had clicked together through the November night and revisiting the out-of-the-way places to which they had driven in her white car. Just as Daisy's house had always seemed to him more mysterious and gay than other houses so his idea of the city itself, even though she was gone from it, was pervaded with a melancholy beauty.

He left feeling that if he had searched harder he might have found her—that he was leaving her behind. The day-coach—he was penniless now—was hot. He went out to the open vestibule and sat down on a folding chair, and the station slid away and the backs of unfamiliar buildings moved by. Then out into the spring fields, where a yellow trolley raced them for a minute with people in it who might once have seen the pale magic of her face along the casual street.

The track curved and now it was going away from the sun which, as it sank lower, seemed to spread itself in benediction over the vanishing city where she had drawn her breath. He stretched out his hand desperately as if to snatch only a wisp of air, to save a fragment of the spot that she had made lovely for him. But it was all going by too fast now for his blurred eyes and he knew that he had lost that part of it, the freshest and the best, forever.

It was nine o'clock when we finished breakfast and went out on the porch. The night had made a sharp difference in the weather and there was an autumn flavor in the air. The gardener, the last one of Gatsby's former servants, came to the foot of the steps.

"I'm going to drain the pool today, Mr. Gatsby. Leaves'll start falling pretty soon and then there's always trouble with the pipes."

"Don't do it today," Gatsby answered. He turned to me apologetically. "You know, old sport, I've never used that pool all summer?"

I looked at my watch and stood up.

"Twelve minutes to my train."

I didn't want to go to the city. I wasn't worth a decent stroke of work but it was more than that—I didn't want to leave Gatsby. I missed that train, and then another, before I could get myself away.

"I'll call you up," I said finally.

"Do, old sport."

"I'll call you about noon."

We walked slowly down the steps.

"I suppose Daisy'll call too." He looked at me anxiously as if he hoped I'd corroborate this.

"I suppose so."

"Well—goodbye."

We shook hands and I started away. Just before I reached the hedge I remembered something and turned around.

"They're a rotten crowd," I shouted, across the lawn. "You're worth the whole damn bunch put together."

I've always been glad I said that. It was the only compliment I ever gave him, because I disapproved of him from beginning to end. First he nodded politely, and then his face broke into that radiant and understanding smile, as if we'd been in ecstatic cahoots on that fact all the time. His gorgeous pink rag of a suit made a bright spot of color against the white steps and I thought of the night when I first came to his ancestral home three months before. The lawn and drive had been crowded with the faces of those who guessed at his corruption—and he had stood on those steps, concealing his incorruptible dream, as he waved them goodbye.

I thanked him for his hospitality. We were always thanking him for that—I and the others.

"Goodbye," I called. "I enjoyed breakfast, Gatsby."

Up in the city I tried for a while to list the quotations on an interminable amount of stock, then I fell asleep in my swivel chair. Just before noon the phone woke me and I started up with sweat breaking out on my forehead. It was Jordan Baker; she often called me up at this hour because the uncertainty of her own movements between hotels and clubs and private houses made her hard to find in any other way. Usually her voice came over the wire as something fresh and cool as if a divot from a green golf links had come sailing in at the office window but this morning it seemed harsh and dry.

"I've left Daisy's house," she said. "I'm at Hempstead and I'm going down to Southampton this afternoon."

Probably it had been tactful to leave Daisy's house, but

the act annoyed me and her next remark made me rigid.

"You weren't so nice to me last night."

"How could it have mattered then?"

Silence for a moment. Then—

"However—I want to see you."

"I want to see you too."

"Suppose I don't go to Southampton, and come into town this afternoon?"

"No—I don't think this afternoon."

"Very well."

"It's impossible this afternoon. Various——"

We talked like that for a while and then abruptly we weren't talking any longer. I don't know which of us hung up with a sharp click but I know I didn't care. I couldn't have talked to her across a teatable that day if I never talked to her again in this world.

I called Gatsby's house a few minutes later but the line was busy. I tried four times; finally an exasperated central told me the wire was being kept open for long distance from Detroit. Taking out my time-table I drew a small circle around the three-fifty train. Then I leaned back in my chair and tried to think. It was just noon.

When I passed the ashheaps on the train that morning I had crossed deliberately to the other side of the car. I supposed there'd be a curious crowd around there all day with little boys searching for dark spots in the dust and some garrulous man telling over and over what had happened until it became less and less real even to him and he could tell it no longer and Myrtle Wilson's tragic achievement was forgotten. Now I want to go back a little and tell what happened at the garage after we left there the night before.

They had difficulty in locating the sister, Catherine. She must have broken her rule against drinking that night for when she arrived she was stupid with liquor and unable to understand that the ambulance had already gone to Flushing. When they convinced her of this she immediately fainted as if that was the intolerable part of the affair. Someone kind or curious took her in his car and drove her in the wake of her sister's body.

Until long after midnight a changing crowd lapped up against the front of the garage while George Wilson rocked himself back and forth on the couch inside. For a while the door of the office was open and everyone who came into the garage glanced irresistibly through it. Finally someone said it was a shame and closed the door. Michaelis and several other men were with him—first four or five men, later two or three men. Still later Michaelis had to ask the last stranger to wait there fifteen minutes longer while he went back to his own place and made a pot of coffee. After that he stayed there alone with Wilson until dawn.

About three o'clock the quality of Wilson's incoherent muttering changed—he grew quieter and began to talk about the yellow car. He announced that he had a way of finding out whom the yellow car belonged to, and then he blurted out that a couple of months ago his wife had come from the city with her face bruised and her nose swollen.

But when he heard himself say this he flinched and began to cry "Oh, my God!" again in his groaning voice. Michaelis made a clumsy attempt to distract him.

"How long have you been married, George? Come on

there, try and sit still a minute and answer my question. How long have you been married?"

"Twelve years."

"Ever had any children? Come on, George, sit still—I asked you a question. Did you ever have any children?"

The hard brown beetles kept thudding against the dull light and whenever Michaelis heard a car go tearing along the road outside it sounded to him like the car that hadn't stopped a few hours before. He didn't like to go into the garage because the work bench was stained where the body had been lying so he moved uncomfortably around the office—he knew every object in it before morning—and from time to time sat down beside Wilson trying to keep him more quiet.

"Have you got a church you go to sometimes, George? Maybe even if you haven't been there for a long time? Maybe I could call up the church and get a priest to come over and he could talk to you, see?"

"Don't belong to any."

"You ought to have a church, George, for times like this. You must have gone to church once. Didn't you get married in a church? Listen, George, listen to me. Didn't you get married in a church?"

"That was a long time ago."

The effort of answering broke the rhythm of his rocking—for a moment he was silent. Then the same half knowing, half bewildered look came back into his faded eyes.

"Look in the drawer there," he said, pointing at the desk.

"Which drawer?"

"That drawer—that one."

Michaelis opened the drawer nearest his hand. There was nothing in it but a small expensive dog leash made of leather and braided silver. It was apparently new.

"This?" he inquired, holding it up.

Wilson stared and nodded.

"I found it yesterday afternoon. She tried to tell me about it but I knew it was something funny."

"You mean your wife bought it?"

"She had it wrapped in tissue paper on her bureau."

Michaelis didn't see anything odd in that and he gave Wilson a dozen reasons why his wife might have bought the dog leash. But conceivably Wilson had heard some of these same explanations before, from Myrtle, because he began saying "Oh, my God!" again in a whisper—his comforter left several explanations in the air.

"Then he killed her," said Wilson. His mouth dropped open suddenly.

"Who did?"

"I have a way of finding out."

"You're morbid, George," said his friend. "This has been a strain to you and you don't know what you're saying. You'd better try and sit quiet till morning."

"He murdered her."

"It was an accident, George."

Wilson shook his head. His eyes narrowed and his mouth widened slightly with the ghost of a superior "Hm!"

"I know," he said definitely. "I'm one of these trusting fellas and I don't think any harm to nobody, but when I get to know a thing I know it. It was the man in that car. She ran out to speak to him and he wouldn't stop."

Michaelis had seen this too but it hadn't occurred to him

that there was any special significance in it. He believed that
Mrs. Wilson had been running away from her husband,
rather than trying to stop any particular car.

"How could she of been like that?"

"She's a deep one," said Wilson, as if that answered the
question. "Ah-h-h——"

He began to rock again and Michaelis stood twisting the
leash in his hand.

"Maybe you got some friend that I could telephone for,
George?"

This was a forlorn hope—he was almost sure that Wilson
had no friend: there was not enough of him for his wife. He
was glad a little later when he noticed a change in the room,
a blue quickening by the window, and realized that dawn
wasn't far off. About five o'clock it was blue enough outside
to snap off the light.

Wilson's glazed eyes turned out to the ashheaps, where
small grey clouds took on fantastic shape and scurried here
and there in the faint dawn wind.

"I spoke to her," he muttered, after a long silence. "I told
her she might fool me but she couldn't fool God. I took her
to the window——" With an effort he got up and walked to
the rear window and leaned with his face pressed against it,
"—and I said 'God knows what you've been doing, everything you've been doing. You may fool me but you can't
fool God!' "

Standing behind him Michaelis saw with a shock that he
was looking at the eyes of Doctor T. J. Eckleburg which had
just emerged pale and enormous from the dissolving night.

"God sees everything," repeated Wilson.

"That's an advertisement," Michaelis assured him.

Something made him turn away from the window and look back into the room. But Wilson stood there a long time, his face close to the window pane, nodding into the twilight.

By six o'clock Michaelis was worn out and grateful for the sound of a car stopping outside. It was one of the watchers of the night before who had promised to come back so he cooked breakfast for three which he and the other man ate together. Wilson was quieter now and Michaelis went home to sleep; when he awoke four hours later and hurried back to the garage Wilson was gone.

His movements—he was on foot all the time—were afterward traced to Port Roosevelt and then to Gad's Hill where he bought a sandwich that he didn't eat and a cup of coffee. He must have been tired and walking slowly for he didn't reach Gad's Hill until noon. Thus far there was no difficulty in accounting for his time—there were boys who had seen a man "acting sort of crazy" and motorists at whom he stared oddly from the side of the road. Then for three hours he disappeared from view. The police, on the strength of what he said to Michaelis, that he "had a way of finding out," supposed that he spent that time going from garage to garage thereabouts inquiring for a yellow car. On the other hand no garage man who had seen him ever came forward—and perhaps he had an easier, surer way of finding out what he wanted to know. By half past two he was in West Egg where he asked someone the way to Gatsby's house. So by that time he knew Gatsby's name.

At two o'clock Gatsby put on his bathing suit and left word with the butler that if anyone phoned word was to be brought to him at the pool. He stopped at the garage for a pneumatic mattress that had amused his guests during the summer, and the chauffeur helped him pump it up. Then he gave instructions that the open car wasn't to be taken out under any circumstances—and this was strange because the front right fender needed repair.

Gatsby shouldered the mattress and started for the pool. Once he stopped and shifted it a little and the chauffeur asked him if he needed help, but he shook his head and in a moment disappeared among the yellowing trees.

No telephone message arrived but the butler went without his sleep and waited for it until four o'clock—until long after there was anyone to give it to if it came. I have an idea that Gatsby himself didn't believe it would come and perhaps he no longer cared. If that was true he must have felt that he had lost the old warm world, paid a high price for living too long with a single dream. He must have looked up at an unfamiliar sky through frightening leaves and shivered as he found what a grotesque thing a rose is and how raw the sunlight was upon the scarcely created grass. A new world, material without being real, where poor ghosts, breathing dreams like air, drifted fortuitously about . . . like that ashen, fantastic figure gliding toward him through the amorphous trees.

The chauffeur—he was one of Wolfshiem's protégés—heard the shots—afterward he could only say that he hadn't thought anything much about them. I drove from the station directly to Gatsby's house and my rushing anxiously up the front steps was the first thing that alarmed anyone. But they knew then, I firmly believe. With scarcely a word said, four of us, the chauffeur, butler, gardener and I, hurried down to the pool.

There was a faint, barely perceptible movement of the water as the fresh flow from one end urged its way toward the drain at the other. With little ripples that were hardly the shadows of waves, the laden mattress moved irregularly down the pool. A small gust of wind that scarcely corrugated the surface was enough to disturb its accidental course with its accidental burden. The touch of a cluster of leaves revolved it slowly, tracing, like the leg of a compass, a thin red circle in the water.

It was after we started with Gatsby toward the house that the gardener saw Wilson's body a little way off in the grass, and the holocaust was complete.

CHAPTER IX

♦

After two years I remember the rest of that day, and that night and the next day, only as an endless drill of police and photographers and newspaper men in and out of Gatsby's front door. A rope stretched across the main gate and a policeman by it kept out the curious, but little boys soon discovered that they could enter through my yard and there were always a few of them clustered open-mouthed about the pool. Someone with a positive manner, perhaps a detective, used the expression "mad man" as he bent over Wilson's body that afternoon, and the adventitious authority of his voice set the key for the newspaper reports next morning.

Most of those reports were a nightmare—grotesque, circumstantial, eager and untrue. When Michaelis's testimony at the inquest brought to light Wilson's suspicions of his wife I thought the whole tale would shortly be served up in racy pasquinade—but Catherine, who might have said anything, didn't say a word. She showed a surprising amount of character about it too—looked at the coroner with determined eyes under that corrected brow of hers and swore that her sister had never seen Gatsby, that her sister was completely happy with her husband, that her sister had been into no mischief whatever. She convinced herself of it and cried into her handkerchief as if the very suggestion was more than she could endure. So Wilson was reduced to a man "deranged by grief" in order that the case might remain in its simplest form. And it rested there.

But all this part of it seemed remote and unessential. I found myself on Gatsby's side, and alone. From the moment I telephoned news of the catastrophe to West Egg Village, every surmise about him, and every practical question, was referred to me. At first I was surprised and confused; then as he lay in his house and didn't move or breathe or speak hour upon hour it grew upon me that I was responsible, because no one else was interested—interested, I mean, with that intense personal interest to which everyone has some vague right at the end.

I called up Daisy half an hour after we found him, called her instinctively and without hesitation. But she and Tom had gone away early that afternoon, and taken baggage with them.

"Left no address?"

"No."

"Say when they'd be back?"

"No."

"Any idea where they are? How I could reach them?"

"I don't know. Can't say."

I wanted to get somebody for him. I wanted to go into the room where he lay and reassure him: "I'll get somebody for you, Gatsby. Don't worry. Just trust me and I'll get somebody for you——"

Meyer Wolfshiem's name wasn't in the phone book. The butler gave me his office address on Broadway and I called Information, but by the time I had the number it was long after five and no one answered the phone.

"Will you ring again?"

"I've rung them three times."

"It's very important."

"Sorry. I'm afraid no one's there."

I went back to the drawing room and thought for an instant that they were chance visitors, all these official people who suddenly filled it. But as they drew back the sheet and looked at Gatsby with unmoved eyes, his protest continued in my brain.

"Look here, old sport, you've got to get somebody for me. You've got to try hard. I can't go through this alone."

Someone started to ask me questions but I broke away and going upstairs looked hastily through the unlocked parts of his desk—he'd never told me definitely that his parents were dead. But there was nothing—only the picture of Dan Cody, a token of forgotten violence staring down from the wall.

Next morning I sent the butler to New York with a letter to Wolfshiem which asked for information and urged him to come out on the next train. That request seemed superfluous when I wrote it. I was sure he'd start when he saw the newspapers, just as I was sure there'd be a wire from Daisy before noon—but neither a wire nor Mr. Wolfshiem arrived, no one arrived, except more police and photographers and newspaper men. When the butler brought back Wolfshiem's answer I began to have a feeling of defiance, of scornful solidarity between Gatsby and me against them all.

Dear Mr. Carraway.   This has been one of the most terrible shocks of my life to me I hardly can believe it that it is true at all. Such a mad act as that man did should make us all think, I cannot come down now as I am tied up in some very important business and cannot get mixed up in this thing now. If there is anything I can do a little later let me know in a letter by Edgar. I hardly know where I am when I hear about a thing like this and am completely knocked down and out.

Yours Truly

MEYER WOLFSHIEM

and then hasty addenda beneath:

Let me know about the funeral etc do not know his family at all.

When the phone rang that afternoon and Long Distance said Chicago was calling I thought this would be Daisy at last. But the connection came through as a man's voice, very thin and far away.

"This is Slagle speaking. . . . "

"Yes?" The name was unfamiliar.

"Hell of a note, isn't it? Get my wire?"

"There haven't been any wires."

"Young Parke's in trouble," he said rapidly. "They picked him up when he handed the bonds over the counter. They got a circular from New York giving 'em the numbers just five minutes before. What d'you know about that, hey? You never can tell in these hick towns——"

"Hello!" I interrupted breathlessly. "Look here—this isn't Mr. Gatsby. Mr. Gatsby's dead."

There was a long silence on the other end of the wire followed by an exclamation . . . then a quick squawk as the connection was broken.

I think it was on the third day that a telegram signed Henry C. Gatz arrived from a town in Minnesota. It said only that the sender was leaving immediately and to postpone the funeral until he came.

It was Gatsby's father, a solemn old man very helpless and dismayed, bundled up in a long cheap ulster against the warm September day. His eyes leaked continuously with excitement and when I took the bag and umbrella from his hands he began to pull so incessantly at his sparse grey beard that I had difficulty in getting off his coat. He was on the point of collapse so I took him into the music room and made him sit down while I sent for something to eat. But he wouldn't eat and the glass of milk spilled from his trembling hand.

"I saw it in the Chicago newspaper," he said. "It was all in the Chicago newspaper. I started right away."

"I didn't know how to reach you."

His eyes, seeing nothing, moved ceaselessly about the room.

"It was a mad man," he said. "He must have been mad."

"Wouldn't you like some coffee?" I urged him.

"I don't want anything. I'm all right now, Mr.——"

"Carraway."

"Well, I'm all right now. Where have they got Jimmy?"

I took him into the drawing room where his son lay, and left him there. Some little boys had come up on the steps and were looking into the hall; when I told them who had arrived they went reluctantly away.

After a little while Mr. Gatz opened the door and came out, his mouth ajar, his face flushed slightly, his eyes leaking isolated and unpunctual tears. He had reached an age where death no longer has the quality of ghastly surprise, and when he looked around him now for the first time and saw the height and splendor of the hall and the great rooms opening out from it into other rooms his grief began to be mixed with an awed pride. I helped him to a bedroom upstairs; while he took off his coat and vest I told him that all arrangements had been deferred until he came.

"I didn't know what you'd want, Mr. Gatsby——"

"Gatz is my name."

"——Mr. Gatz. I thought you might want to take the body west."

He shook his head.

"Jimmy always liked it better down East. He rose up to his position in the East. Were you a friend of my boy's, Mr.——?"

"We were close friends."

"He had a big future before him, you know. He was only a young man but he had a lot of brain power here."

He touched his head impressively and I nodded.

"If he'd of lived he'd of been a great man. A man like James J. Hill. He'd of helped build up the country."

"That's true," I said uncomfortably.

He fumbled at the embroidered coverlet, trying to take it from the bed, and lay down stiffly—was instantly asleep.

That night an obviously frightened person called up and demanded to know who I was before he would give his name.

"This is Mr. Carraway," I said.

"Oh—" He sounded relieved. "This is Klipspringer."

I was relieved too for that seemed to promise another friend at Gatsby's grave. I didn't want it to be in the papers and draw a sightseeing crowd so I'd been calling up a few people myself. They were hard to find.

"The funeral's tomorrow," I said. "Three o'clock here at the house. I wish you'd tell anybody who'd be interested."

"Oh, I will," he broke out hastily. "Of course I'm not likely to see anybody, but if I do."

His tone made me suspicious.

"Of course you'll be there yourself."

"Well, I'll certainly try. What I called up about is——"

"Wait a minute," I interrupted. "How about saying you'll come?"

"Well, the fact is—the truth of the matter is that I'm staying with some people up here in Greenwich and they rather expect me to be with them tomorrow. In fact there's a sort of picnic or something. Of course I'll do my very best to get away."

I ejaculated an unrestrained "Huh!" and he must have heard me for he went on nervously:

"What I called up about was a pair of shoes I left there. I wonder if it'd be too much trouble to have the butler send them on. You see they're tennis shoes and I'm sort of helpless without them. My address is care of B. F.——"

I didn't hear the rest of the name because I hung up the receiver.

After that I felt a certain shame for Gatsby—one gentleman to whom I telephoned implied that he had got what he deserved. However, that was my fault, for he was one of those who used to sneer most bitterly at Gatsby on the courage of Gatsby's liquor and I should have known better than to call him.

The morning of the funeral I went up to New York to see Meyer Wolfshiem; I couldn't seem to reach him any other way. The door that I pushed open on the advice of an elevator boy was marked "The Swastika Holding Company" and at first there didn't seem to be anyone inside. But when I'd shouted "Hello" several times in vain an argument broke out behind a partition and presently a lovely Jewess appeared at an interior door and scrutinized me with black hostile eyes.

"Nobody's in," she said. "Mr. Wolfshiem's gone to Chicago."

The first part of this was obviously untrue for someone had begun to whistle "The Rosary," tunelessly, inside.

"Please say that Mr. Carraway wants to see him."

"I can't get him back from Chicago, can I?"

At this moment a voice unmistakably Wolfshiem's called "Stella!" from the other side of the door.

"Leave your name on the desk," she said quickly. "I'll give it to him when he gets back."

"But I know he's there."

She took a step toward me and began to slide her hands indignantly up and down her hips.

"You young men think you can force your way in here any time," she scolded. "We're getting sickantired of it. When I say he's in Chicago he's in Chicago."

I mentioned Gatsby.

"Oh-h!" She looked at me over again. "Will you just—— what was your name?"

She vanished. In a moment Meyer Wolfshiem stood solemnly in the doorway, holding out both hands. He drew me into his office, remarking in a reverent voice that it was a sad time for all of us, and offered me a cigar.

"My memory goes back to when first I met him," he said. "A young major just out of the army and covered over with medals he got in the war. He was so hard up he had to keep on wearing his uniform because he couldn't buy some regular clothes. First time I saw him was when he come into Winebrenner's poolroom at Forty-third Street and asked for a job. He hadn't eat anything for a couple of days. 'Come on have some lunch with me,' I sid. He ate more than four dollars' worth of food in half an hour."

"Did you start him in business?" I inquired.

"Start him! I made him."

"Oh."

"I raised him up out of nothing, right out of the gutter. I saw right away he was a fine appearing gentlemanly young man and when he told me he was an Oggsford I knew I could use him good. I got him to join up in the American Legion and he used to stand high there. Right off he did some work for a client of mine up to Albany. We were so thick like that in everything—" He held up two bulbous fingers "—always together."

I wondered if this partnership had included the World's Series transaction in 1919.

"Now he's dead," I said after a moment. "You were his closest friend, so I know you'll want to come to his funeral this afternoon."

"I'd like to come."

"Well, come then."

The hair in his nostrils quivered slightly and as he shook his head his eyes filled with tears.

"I can't do it—I can't get mixed up in it," he said.

"There's nothing to get mixed up in. It's all over now."

"When a man gets killed I never like to get mixed up in it in any way. I keep out. When I was a young man it was different—if a friend of mine died, no matter how, I stuck with them to the end. You may think that's sentimental but I mean it—to the bitter end."

I saw that for some reason of his own he was determined not to come, so I stood up.

"Are you a college man?" he inquired suddenly.

For a moment I thought he was going to suggest a "gonnegtion" but he only nodded and shook my hand.

"Let us learn to show our friendship for a man when he is alive and not after he is dead," he suggested. "After that my own rule is to let everything alone."

When I left his office the sky had turned dark and I got back to West Egg in a drizzle. After changing my clothes I went next door and found Mr. Gatz walking up and down excitedly in the hall. His pride in his son and in his son's possessions was continually increasing and now he had something to show me.

"Jimmy sent me this picture." He took out his wallet with trembling fingers. "Look there."

It was a photograph of the house, cracked in the corners and dirty with many hands. He pointed out every detail to me eagerly. "Look there!" and then sought admiration from my eyes. He had shown it so often that I think it was more real to him now than the house itself.

"Jimmy sent it to me. I think it's a very pretty picture. It shows up well."

"Very well. Had you seen him lately?"

"He come out to see me two years ago and bought me the house I live in now. Of course we was broke up when he run off from home but I see now there was a reason for it. He knew he had a big future in front of him. And ever since he made a success he was very generous with me."

He seemed reluctant to put away the picture, held it for another minute, lingeringly, before my eyes. Then he returned the wallet and pulled from his pocket a ragged old copy of a book called "Hopalong Cassidy."

"Look here, this is a book he had when he was a boy. It just shows you."

He opened it at the back cover and turned it around for me to see. On the last fly-leaf was printed the word SCHEDULE, and the date September 12th, 1906. And underneath:

Rise from bed	6.00	A.M.
Dumbbell exercise and wall-scaling	6.15–6.30	"
Study electricity, etc.	7.15–8.15	"
Work	8.30–4.30	P.M.
Baseball and sports	4.30–5.00	"
Practice elocution, poise and how to		
attain it	5.00–6.00	"
Study needed inventions	7.00–9.00	"

GENERAL RESOLVES

No wasting time at Shafters or [a name, indecipherable]
No more smokeing or chewing

Bath every other day
Read one improving book or magazine per week
Save $5.00 [crossed out] $3.00 per week
Be better to parents

"I come across this book by accident," said the old man. "It just shows you, don't it?"

"It just shows you."

"Jimmy was bound to get ahead. He always had some resolves like this or something. Do you notice what he's got about improving his mind? He was always great for that. He told me I et like a hog once and I beat him for it."

He was reluctant to close the book, reading each item aloud and then looking eagerly at me. I think he rather expected me to copy down the list for my own use.

A little before three the Lutheran minister arrived from Flushing and I began to look involuntarily out the windows for other cars. So did Gatsby's father. And as the time passed and the servants came in and stood waiting in the hall his eyes began to blink anxiously and he spoke of the rain in a worried uncertain way. The minister glanced several times at his watch so I took him aside and asked him to wait for half an hour. But it wasn't any use. Nobody came.

About five o'clock our procession of three cars reached the cemetery and stopped in a thick drizzle beside the gate—first a motor hearse, horribly black and wet, then Mr. Gatz and the minister and I in the limousine, and, a little later, four or five servants and the postman from West Egg in Gatsby's station wagon, all wet to the skin. As we started through the gate into the cemetery I heard a car stop and then the sound of someone splashing after us over the soggy ground. I looked around. It was the man with owl-eyed glasses whom I had found marvelling over Gatsby's books in the library one night three months before.

I'd never seen him since then. I don't know how he knew about the funeral or even his name. The rain poured down his thick glasses and he took them off and wiped them to see the protecting canvas unrolled from Gatsby's grave.

I tried to think about Gatsby then for a moment but he was already too far away and I could only remember, without resentment, that Daisy hadn't sent a message or a flower. Dimly I heard someone murmur "Blessed are the dead that the rain falls on," and then the owl-eyed man said "Amen to that," in a brave voice.

We straggled down quickly through the rain to the cars. Owl Eyes spoke to me by the gate.

"I couldn't get to the house," he remarked.

"Neither could anybody else."

"Go on!" He started. "Why, my God! they used to go there by the hundreds."

He took off his glasses and wiped them again outside and in.

"The poor son-of-a-bitch," he said.

`One of my most vivid memories is of coming back west from prep school and later from college at Christmas time. Those who went farther than Chicago would gather in the old dim Union Station at six o'clock of a December evening with a few Chicago friends already caught up into their own holiday gayeties to bid them a hasty goodbye. I remember the fur coats of the girls returning from Miss This or That's and the chatter of frozen breath and the hands waving overhead as we caught sight of old acquaintances and the matchings of invitations: "Are you going to the Ordways'? the Herseys'? the Schultzes'?" and the long green tickets clasped tight in our gloved hands. And last the murky yellow cars of the Chicago, Milwaukee & St. Paul Railroad looking cheerful as Christmas itself on the tracks beside the gate.

When we pulled out into the winter night and the real snow, our snow, began to stretch out beside us and twinkle against the windows, and the dim lights of small Wisconsin stations moved by, a sharp wild brace came suddenly into the air. We drew in deep breaths of it as we walked back from dinner through the cold vestibules, unutterably aware of our identity with this country for one strange hour before we melted indistinguishably into it again.

That's my middle-west—not the wheat or the prairies or the lost Swede towns but the thrilling, returning trains of my youth and the street lamps and sleigh bells in the frosty dark and the shadows of holly wreaths thrown by lighted windows on the snow. I am part of that, a little solemn with the feel of those long winters, a little complacent from growing up in the Carraway house in a city where dwellings are still called through decades by a family's name. I see now that this has been a story of the West, after all—Tom and Gatsby, Daisy and Jordan and I, were all Westerners, and perhaps we possessed some deficiency in common which made us subtly unadaptable to Eastern life.

Even when the East excited me most, even when I was most keenly aware of its superiority to the bored, sprawling, swollen towns beyond the Ohio, with their interminable inquisitions which spared only the children and the very old—even then it had always for me a quality of distortion. West Egg especially still figures in my more fantastic dreams. I see it as a night scene by El Greco: a hundred houses, at once conventional and grotesque, crouching under a sullen, overhanging sky and a lustreless moon. In the foreground four solemn men in dress suits are walking along the sidewalk with a stretcher on which lies a drunken woman in a white evening dress. Her hand, which dangles over the side, sparkles cold with jewels. Gravely the men turn in at a house—the wrong house. But no one knows the woman's name, and no one cares.

After Gatsby's death the East was haunted for me like that, distorted beyond my eyes' power of correction. So when the blue smoke of brittle leaves was in the air and the wind blew the wet laundry stiff on the line I decided to come back home.

There was one thing to be done before I left, an awkward, unpleasant thing that perhaps had better have been let alone. But I wanted to leave things in order and not just trust that obliging and indifferent sea to sweep my refuse away. I saw Jordan Baker and talked over and around what had happened to us together and what had happened after-ward to me, and she lay perfectly still listening in a big chair.

She was dressed to play golf and I remember thinking she looked like a good illustration, her chin raised a little, jaun-tily, her hair the color of an autumn leaf, her face the same brown tint as the fingerless glove on her knee. When I had finished she told me without comment that she was engaged to another man. I doubted that though there were several she could have married at a nod of her head but I pretended to be surprised. For just a minute I wondered if I wasn't making a mistake, then I thought it all over again quickly and got up to say goodbye.

"Nevertheless you did throw me over," said Jordan suddenly. "You threw me over on the telephone. I don't give a damn about you now but it was a new experience for me and I felt a little dizzy for a while."

We shook hands.

"Oh, and do you remember—" she added, "—a conversation we had once about driving a car?"

"Why,—not exactly."

"You said a bad driver was only safe until she met another bad driver? Well, I met another bad driver, didn't I? I mean it was careless of me to make such a wrong guess. I thought you were rather an honest, straightforward person. I thought it was your secret pride."

"I'm thirty," I said. "I'm five years too old to lie to myself and call it honor."

She didn't answer. Angry, and half in love with her, and tremendously sorry, I turned away.

One afternoon late in October I saw Tom Buchanan. He was walking ahead of me along Fifth Avenue in his alert, aggressive way, his hands out a little from his body as if to fight off interference, his head moving sharply here and there, adapting itself to his restless eyes. Just as I slowed up to avoid overtaking him he stopped and began frowning into the windows of a jewelry store. Suddenly he saw me and walked back holding out his hand.

"What's the matter, Nick? Do you object to shaking hands with me?"

"Yes. You know what I think of you."

"You're crazy, Nick," he said quickly. "Crazy as hell. I don't know what's the matter with you."

"Tom," I inquired, "what did you say to Wilson that afternoon?"

He stared at me without a word and I knew I had guessed right about those missing hours. I started to turn away but he took a step after me and grabbed my arm.

"I told him the truth," he said. "He came to the door while we were getting ready to leave and when I sent down word that we weren't in he tried to force his way upstairs. He was crazy enough to kill me if I hadn't told him who owned the car. His hand was on a revolver in his pocket every minute he was in the house——" He broke off defiantly. "What if I did tell him? That fellow had it coming to him. He threw dust into your eyes just like he did in Daisy's but he was a tough one. He ran over Myrtle like you'd run over a dog and never even stopped his car."

There was nothing I could say, except the one unutterable fact that it wasn't true.

"And if you think I didn't have my share of suffering—look here, when I went to give up that flat and saw that damn box of dog biscuits sitting there on the sideboard I sat down and cried like a baby. By God it was awful——"

I couldn't forgive him or like him but I saw that what he had done was, to him, entirely justified. It was all very careless and confused. They were careless people, Tom and Daisy—they smashed up things and creatures and then retreated back into their money or their vast carelessness or whatever it was that kept them together, and let other people clean up the mess they had made . . . .

I shook hands with him; it seemed silly not to, for I felt suddenly as though I were talking to a child. Then he went into the jewelry store to buy a pearl necklace—or perhaps only a pair of cuff buttons—rid of my provincial squeamishness forever.

Gatsby's house was still empty when I left—the grass on his lawn had grown as long as mine. One of the taxi drivers in the village never took a fare past the entrance gate without stopping for a minute and pointing inside; perhaps it was he who drove Daisy and Gatsby over to East Egg the night of the accident and perhaps he had made a story about it all his own. I didn't want to hear it and I avoided him when I got off the train.

I spent my Saturday nights in New York because those gleaming, dazzling parties of his were with me so vividly that I could still hear the music and the laughter faint and incessant from his garden and the cars going up and down his drive. One night I did hear a material car there and saw its lights stop at his front steps. But I didn't investigate. Probably it was some final guest who had been away at the ends of the earth and didn't know that the party was over.

On the last night, with my trunk packed and my car sold to the grocer, I went over and looked at that huge incoherent failure of a house once more. On the white steps an obscene word, scrawled by some boy with a piece of brick, stood out clearly in the moonlight and I erased it, drawing my shoe raspingly along the stone. Then I wandered down to the beach and sprawled out on the sand.

Most of the big shore places were closed now and there were hardly any lights except the shadowy, moving glow of a ferryboat across the Sound. And as the moon rose higher the inessential houses began to melt away until gradually I became aware of the old island here that flowered once for Dutch sailors' eyes—a fresh, green breast of the new world. Its vanished trees, the trees that had made way for Gatsby's house, had once pandered in whispers to the last and greatest of all human dreams; for a transitory enchanted moment man must have held his breath in the presence of this continent, compelled into an æsthetic contemplation he neither understood nor desired, face to face for the last time in history with something commensurate to his capacity for wonder.

And as I sat there, brooding on the old unknown world, I thought of Gatsby's wonder when he first picked out the green light at the end of Daisy's dock. He had come a long way to this blue lawn and his dream must have seemed so close that he could hardly fail to grasp it. He did not know that it was already behind him, somewhere back in that vast obscurity beyond the city, where the dark fields of the republic rolled on under the night.

Gatsby believed in the green light, the orgastic future that year by year recedes before us. It eluded us then, but that's no matter—tomorrow we will run faster, stretch out our arms farther. . . . And one fine morning——

So we beat on, boats against the current, borne back ceaselessly into the past.

The Text of *The Great Gatsby*

by Matthew J. Bruccoli

♦

Innocent readers assume that the printed texts of a classic are trustworthy. Their confidence is too often betrayed. The history of the republication of most standard works of literature is a record of increasing departure from a first printing that may not have been an accurate publication of what the author expected to see printed.

This volume provides the established text of *The Great Gatsby* from the 1991 Cambridge University Press critical edition—the first accurate text of a masterpiece that has been published and republished in flawed texts. The first edition (New York: Charles Scribner's Sons, 1925) was blemished, and subsequent editions have introduced further corruption.

The textual errors in *The Great Gatsby* resulted from a compound of causes: Fitzgerald's custom of revising and rewriting in proof made for a rushed production schedule; his spelling was idiosyncratic; he had difficulty with details of geography and arithmetic; he relied on his editor, Maxwell Perkins, to check his work; he was in Italy while the novel was being edited and printed—in the days before airmail.

Because Fitzgerald was a saver of working drafts, many

of his intentions can be recovered by a study of the surviving manuscripts, the rewritten galleys, and his marked copy of *Gatsby*. The present text corrects or revises seventy-four of the substantive or word readings in the first printing. For example, the age of Daisy's daughter has been corrected from three to two years, obviating the false inference that Daisy was pregnant at the time of her wedding (p. 14, line 17). On page 40, line 8, the restoration of Fitzgerald's word *was* for the incorrect first-edition reading *saw* emphasizes Nick's capacity to imaginatively project himself into the experiences he observes: "Yet high over the city our line of yellow windows must have contributed their share of human secrecy to the casual watcher in the darkening streets, and I was him too, looking up and wondering." When Edmund Wilson re-edited the novel after Fitzgerald's death, he tampered with the eloquent coda: "Gatsby believed in the green light, the orgastic future . . ." substituting *orgiastic* for *orgastic* (p. 189, line 24).

Factual errors in fiction distract readers who spot them and may undermine confidence in the work and the author.* Many careful readers hold that if an author cannot be trusted in details, he may not be trustworthy in larger matters. This concern bears on Fitzgerald's fiction, which delicately evokes the nuances of time and place—but errs in details of chronology and geography. He was an impressionistic realist—not a reportorial or documentary realist. As a social historian, Fitzgerald utilized real places and real details for the denotations and connotations these references generated in informed readers: thus the Gatsby-Tom confrontation is set in the Plaza Hotel—after two other locations were rejected—to take advantage of the associations of this actual hotel. As an impressionist, Fitzgerald sought to convey, by means of language and style, the emotions associated with actual and fictional settings.

Not all factual errors are inadvertent; some putative errors are—or may be—deliberate and meaningful. For example, Gatsby's claim to be a Midwesterner from San Francisco indicates his autobiographical untrustworthiness; but readers have regarded it as Fitzgerald's error—not as Gatsby's blunder. Other errors in the novel have fueled controversy over Nick Carraway's reliability as a narrator—for example, the chronological inconsistencies.

The factual errors in *The Great Gatsby* are divisible into external errors (those regarding the actual outside world in which the novel is set) and internal errors (those involving the fictional world of the novel). The external errors in the novel resulted from a combination of circumstances: Fitzgerald's shaky geography, his residence in Europe while writing the novel, and the haste with which the book was manufactured. He was not always scrupulous about real details, but there is evidence that Fitzgerald attempted to get them right. He made factual corrections or revisions in his copy of the novel. Nonetheless, Fitzgerald was incapable of factual meticulosity, although he took pains with stylistic revisions.

There are two geographies of *The Great Gatsby:* the fictional geography imposed on Long Island (East Egg and West Egg) and the actual New York City. Fitzgerald's invented geography has not been editorially altered; however, his mistakes in actual geography have required difficult decisions. Because *The Great Gatsby* has become an international source for American social history and is read as a record of American life at an actual time and place, non-functional factual mistakes have been corrected in this text; those which are uncorrected or uncorrectable are explained in the notes.

External errors have been corrected in the text of this edition wherever the emendations could be made by simple substitution. Internal errors have been corrected when they are clearly inadvertent and threaten to distract the reader. No emendations requiring rewriting have been made. Certain internal errors or inconsistencies—mainly chronological—have been retained because they are embedded in the fabric of the work or because correction would exceed the proper limits of editorial authority.

Of particular importance is the recovery in this text of four space breaks (pp. 110, 115, 161, 178), by which Fitzgerald signaled shifts in time or narrative—significant matters in a complexly structured novel. This text also restores some 1,100 of Fitzgerald's punctuation marks. Punctuation is not decoration: a few commas more or less do not matter much in a novel, but more than a thousand punctuation interferences alter the overall rhythm of the prose—a serious matter in reading a stylist whose sense for the sound and movement of the American language has been compared to perfect pitch. In general, the editorial process has removed the commas editorially supplied in 1925—which slow the pace of Fitzgerald's lighter "ear punctuation." Thus in the third paragraph, this text removes seven non-authorial commas and restores one Fitzgerald dash—a punctuation mark that he used deliberately.

---

*Bruccoli, "Getting It Right: The Publishing Process and the Correction of Factual Errors—With Reference to *The Great Gatsby*," *Library Chronicle of the University of Texas at Austin*, 21, no. 3-4 (1991), 41–60.

Publisher's Afterword

♦

More than sixty-five years since its publication, *The Great Gatsby* stands as F. Scott Fitzgerald's masterpiece and indeed as a preeminent masterpiece of twentieth-century American literature. Today it is studied in high schools and colleges across the land, where more copies of this paperback edition are now sold annually than the *total* cumulative sale of all editions published throughout the author's lifetime. I was once asked whether Fitzgerald himself would have been surprised by *Gatsby*'s fate. Perhaps not. His immediate hope, of course, was to write a thoroughly contemporary novel about American society in the Twenties and, at the same time, another instant success like his first novel, *This Side of Paradise* (1920). Yet he might not be so startled today to discover that his book had transcended its own age and turned into a timeless classic, for he had wanted it to be—in his own words—a "consciously artistic achievement." *Gatsby* has simply lived up to the author's expectations.

As early as the summer of 1922, when Fitzgerald was just beginning to conceive the novel, he confessed to his editor, Maxwell Perkins at Scribners, that he wanted to break new ground as a writer. He was determined to write something quite different from his two earlier, loosely constructed and unabashedly semi-autobiographical novels, *This Side of Paradise* and *The Beautiful and Damned* (1922). He began work on the new novel a year later, in the summer of 1923, while living in Great Neck, Long Island. But he was preoccupied with rehearsals of his ill-starred comedy *The Vegetable—or from President to postman*. After the dramatic failure of *The Vegetable,* Fitzgerald temporarily abandoned work on *Gatsby*. In an attempt to recoup his financial losses, he turned out a spate of short stories. In April 1924 he wrote to Perkins that he was returning in earnest to his novel, this time working on a "new angle."

Maxwell Perkins, who embodied both the voice and literary conscience of Scribners, was clearly elated. His great expectations—and equal impatience—for the delivery of Fitzgerald's new novel prompted Perkins immediately to commission (seven months in advance of the finished manuscript, as it would turn out) a full-color, illustrated dust jacket to be held in readiness for the new book.

The artist chosen was the Spanish-born Francis Cugat, who had designed posters and movie sets in New York before he became an art designer in Hollywood for Douglas Fairbanks. His painting, here reproduced on the cover, is the most celebrated—and widely disseminated—jacket art in twentieth-century American literature. Like the novel it embellishes, this Art Deco tour de force has firmly established itself as a classic. At the same time, it represents a unique form of "collaboration" between author and jacket artist. Under normal circumstances, the artist illustrates a scene or motif conceived by the author; he lifts, as it were, his image from a page of the book. In this instance, however, the artist's image *preceded* the finished manuscript and Fitzgerald actually maintained that he had "written it into" his book.

Cugat's rendition is not illustrative, but symbolic, even iconic: the sad, hypnotic, heavily outlined eyes of a woman beam like headlights through a cobalt night sky. Their irises are transfigured into reclining female nudes. From one of the eyes streams a green luminescent tear; brightly rouged lips complete the sensual triangle. Below, on earth, colored carnival lights blaze before a metropolitan skyline.

It has been alleged that Fitzgerald's symbolic billboard eyes of Doctor T. J. Eckleburg derived from Cugat's jacket art. Fitzgerald describes them as "blue and gigantic—their retinas are one yard high. They look out of no face, but, instead, from a pair of enormous yellow spectacles which pass over a non-existent nose." If this hypothetical source is valid, then we are clearly not dealing here with a literal translation from graphic imagery into prose: there can be no mistaking of Cugat's seductive visage for the grotesque, bespectacled eyes of the optician's billboard. Yet each image is, in its own way, both ethereal and mystical; each is explicitly abstracted from a face, in each case with the nose "edited out." As we would expect from a writer of Fitzgerald's imagination, he thoroughly transforms his visual sources, or background images, into his own creation: that is to say, one symbol *evolves* into another.

An alternative textual reference is Nick Carraway's image of Daisy as the "girl whose disembodied face floated along the dark cornices and blinding signs" of nighttime New York at the close of chapter four. Still more possibilities are prompted

by Matthew J. Bruccoli's recent discovery of Cugat's preparatory studies and sketches for the final jacket, which begin
with a scene of the "valley of ashes" over which hover ghostly
apparitions of sorrowful female faces—a series of sad, celestial eyes that the artist was to transform and clarify through
subsequent sketches.* The locale eventually was shifted to
the Manhattan skyline, which in turn was relegated to a
backdrop for the pyrotechnical lights of Coney Island.
Cugat's carnival imagery is especially intriguing in view of
Fitzgerald's pervasive use of light motifs throughout his
novel; specifically, in metaphors for the latter-day Trimalchio, whose parties were illuminated by "enough colored
lights to make a Christmas tree of Gatsby's enormous garden." Nick sees "the whole corner of the peninsula . . . blazing
with light" from Gatsby's house "lit from tower to cellar."
When he tells Gatsby that his place "looks like the world's
fair," Gatsby proposes that they "go to Coney Island."

Daisy's face, says Nick, was "sad and lovely with bright
things in it, bright eyes and a bright passionate mouth." In
Cugat's final painting, her celestial eyes enclose reclining
nudes and her streaming tear is green—like the light "that
burns all night" at the end of her dock, reflected in the water
of the Sound that separates her from Gatsby. What Fitzgerald in fact extracted from Cugat's art and "wrote into"
the novel must, of course, remain an open question. What
is beyond doubt is that Perkins hit the mark when, having
finally read the completed typescript, he declared the jacket
"a masterpiece."

---

*For a full analysis of the preparatory artwork, see Scribner, "Celestial
Eyes—from Metamorphosis to Masterpiece," in *Princeton University Library Chronicle*, LIII, No. 2, Winter 1992.

Perhaps nowhere is Perkins's elusive editorial genius more concrete than in his long report to Fitzgerald in late November, after he had read and thoroughly digested the manuscript:

> I think you have every kind of right to be proud of this book. It is an extraordinary book, suggestive of all sorts of thoughts and moods. You adopted exactly the right method of telling it, that of employing a narrator who is more of a spectator than an actor: this puts the reader upon a point of observation on a higher level than that on which the characters stand and at a distance that gives perspective. In no other way could your irony have been so immensely effective, nor the reader have been enabled so strongly to feel at times the strangeness of human circumstance in a vast heedless universe. In the eyes of Dr. Eckleburg various readers will see different significances; but their presence gives a superb touch to the whole thing: great unblinking eyes, expressionless, looking down upon the human scene. It's magnificent!
>
> I could go on praising the book and speculating on its various elements, and meanings, but points of criticism are more important now. I think you are right in feeling a certain slight sagging in chapters six and seven, and I don't know how to suggest a remedy. I hardly doubt that you will find one and I am only writing to say that I think it does need something to hold up here to the pace set, and ensuing. I have only two actual criticisms:—
>
> One is that among a set of characters marvelously palpable and vital—I would know Tom Buchanan if I met him on the street and would avoid him—Gatsby is somewhat vague. The reader's eyes can never quite focus upon him, his outlines are

dim. Now everything about Gatsby is more or less a mystery i.e. more or less vague, and this may be somewhat of an artistic intention, but I think it is mistaken. Couldn't *he* be physically described as distinctly as the others, and couldn't you add one or two characteristics like the use of that phrase "old sport,"— not verbal, but physical ones, perhaps. I think that for some reason or other a reader—this was true of Mr. Scribner and of Louise—gets an idea that Gatsby is a much older man than he is, although you have the writer say that he is little older than himself. But this would be avoided if on his first appearance he was seen as vividly as Daisy and Tom are, for instance;—and I do not think your scheme would be impaired if you made him so.

The other point is also about Gatsby: his career must remain mysterious, of course. But in the end you make it pretty clear that his wealth came through his connection with Wolfsheim. You also suggest this much earlier. Now almost all readers numerically are going to be puzzled by his having all this wealth and are going to feel entitled to an explanation. To give a distinct and definite one would be, of course, utterly absurd. It did occur to me though, that you might here and there interpolate some phrases, and possibly incidents, little touches of various kinds, that would suggest that he was in some active way mysteriously engaged. You do have him called on the telephone, but couldn't he be seen once or twice consulting at his parties with people of some sort of mysterious significance, from the political, the gambling, the sporting world, or what-ever it may be. I know I am floundering, but that fact may help you to see what I mean. The *total* lack of an explanation through so large a part of the story does seem to me a defect;—or not of an explanation, but of the suggestion of an explanation. I wish you were here so I could talk about it to you for then I know I could at least make you understand what I mean. What Gatsby did ought never to be definitely imparted, even if it could be. Whether he was an innocent tool in the hands of somebody else, or to what degree he was this, ought not to be explained. But if some sort of business activity of his were simply adumbrated, it would lend further probability to that part of the story.

There is one other point: in giving deliberately Gatsby's biography when he gives it to the narrator you do depart from the method of the narrative in some degree, for otherwise almost everything is told, and beautifully told, in the regular flow of it,—in the succession of events or in accompaniment with them. But you can't avoid the biography altogether. I thought you might find ways to let the truth of some of his claims like "Oxford" and his army career come out bit by bit in the course of actual narrative. I mention the point anyway for consideration in this interval before I send the proofs.

The general brilliant quality of the book makes me ashamed to make even these criticisms. The amount of meaning you get into a sentence, the dimensions and intensity of the impression you make a paragraph carry, are most extraordinary. The manuscript is full of phrases which make a scene blaze with life. If one enjoyed a rapid railroad journey I would compare the number and vividness of pictures your living words suggest, to the living scenes disclosed in that way. It seems in reading a much shorter book than it is, but it carries the mind through a series of experiences that one would think would require a book of three times its length.

The presentation of Tom, his place, Daisy and Jordan, and the unfolding of their characters is unequalled so far as I know.

The description of the valley of ashes adjacent to the lovely country, the conversation and the action in Myrtle's apartment, the marvelous catalogue of those who came to Gatsby's house,—these are such things as make a man famous. And all these things, the whole pathetic episode, you have given a place in time and space, for with the help of T. J. Eckleburg and by an occasional glance at the sky, or the sea, or the city, you have imparted a sort of sense of eternity. You once told me you were not a *natural* writer—my God! You have plainly mastered the craft, of course; but you needed far more than craftsmanship for this.

Several months after the book's publication in April 1925, Fitzgerald gave his editor more than generous credit: "Max," he wrote, "it amuses me when praise comes in on the 'structure' of the book—because it was you who fixed up the structure, not me." Actually the solid foundation and architecture were the author's own achievement. Perkins had merely refined some of the details. He was the gifted mason, not the architect.

The reviews of *Gatsby* were mixed. The first to appear in New York, just two days after publication, was headed F. Scott Fitzgerald's Latest a Dud (the *New York World*). The reviewer for the *Brooklyn Eagle* claimed she could not find "one chemical trace of magic, life, irony, romance or mysticism in all of *The Great Gatsby*" and concluded that "the boy" was "simply puttering around."

Yet there were those, if too few of them, who sensed the greatness in *Gatsby* that would require another generation to be acknowledged. H. L. Mencken, although he found the form "no more than a glorified anecdote," and "a far inferior story at bottom," recognized the novel as "plainly the product of a sound and stable talent, conjured into being by hard work." And he appreciated the craft of revision that accounted for so much: "It shows on every page the results of that laborious effort. . . . There are pages so artfully contrived that one can no more imagine improvising them than one can imagine improvising a fugue." Finally he credits the author with depicting "the rattle and hullabaloo" of society "with great gusto . . . and sharp accuracy." But the critic's crown must go to Gilbert Seldes, who more than anyone else appreciated the author's achievement and articulated the qualities which suggest a classic beneath the surface. "*The Great Gatsby,*" he wrote, "is a brilliant work, and it is also a sound one; it is carefully written, and vivid; it has structure, and it has life. To all the talents, discipline has been added."

Commercially, the novel was a disappointment to Fitzgerald. He had expressed a hope for a sale of 75,000 copies. The first printing of slightly over 20,000 copies sold slowly, however. A second printing of 3,000 copies was put through in August, but the subsequent sales never caught up with it, and when Fitzgerald died fifteen years later there were still unsold copies of that printing in the Scribner warehouse. The novel was never out of print; it had simply stopped selling.

Fitzgerald blamed the commercial failure of his novel on its title ("only fair, rather bad than good") and "*most important,*" he underscored, "the book contains no important woman character and women control the fiction market at present." Today these two explanations seem incredible. Both the title and Daisy Buchanan appear to lie at the very heart of the novel. In an effort to console the despairing Fitzgerald, Perkins responded with a prophecy he did not live to see fulfilled: "One thing I think we can be sure of: that when the tumult and shouting of the rabble of reviewers and gossipers dies, *The Great Gatsby* will stand out as a very extraordinary book."

In 1926 an English edition was published by Chatto and Windus, and in 1934 Scribners licensed *Gatsby* to the Modern Library, a series of inexpensive hardcover reprints. Fitzgerald wrote a preface for that edition which carried the following poignant *apologia pro libro suo:*

> Now that this book is being reissued, the author would like to say that never before did one try to keep his artistic conscience as pure as during the ten months put into doing it. Reading it over one can see how it could have been improved— yet without feeling guilty of any discrepancy from the truth, as far as I saw it; truth or rather the *equivalent* of the truth, the attempt at honesty of imagination. . . . I had recently been kidded half haywire by critics who felt that my material was such as to preclude all dealing with mature persons in a mature world. But, my God! it was my material, and it was all I had to deal with.
>
> What I cut out of it both physically and emotionally would make another novel!

The revival—or, better, the apotheosis—of *Gatsby* began after the author's death. In the volume containing the posthumous publication of Fitzgerald's unfinished novel, *The Last Tycoon,* Scribners included, along with a selection of short stories, *The Great Gatsby.* That was in 1941. It took another five years for a new generation to rediscover it. But the 1950s witnessed a skyrocketing of fame for the novel and Fitzgerald's works in general—an explosion the like of which has rarely been seen in American letters. Book after book was reissued, followed by new collections of stories. By the end of the decade a special student's edition of *Gatsby* was published, reflecting its established place in the academic curriculum. And when, in 1960, the Scribner Library—a series of best-selling classics in paperback—was introduced *The Great Gatsby* was given preeminence: it was labeled "SL 1," and to the present day its place at the top of Scribner bestsellers has never been challenged. This fact, more than any critic's or scholar's sanction, testifies to the book's hallowed place in American literature.

Charles Scribner III
New York, 1992

Long Island: East Egg to Manhattan.

Explanatory Notes

♦

title: *The Great Gatsby*

Fitzgerald was never satisfied with *The Great Gatsby* as the title. The early working title was "Among the Ash Heaps and Million-aires"; other titles that he considered were "Trimalchio in West Egg," "Trimalchio," "On the Road to West Egg," "Gold-hatted Gatsby," and "The High-bouncing Lover." The last two come from the epigraph poem by Fitzgerald, which he attributed to Thomas Parke D'Invilliers, a character in *This Side of Paradise*, his first novel. Trimalchio was the lavish host in *The Satyricon*, a Latin work by Petronius. On 19 March 1925, three weeks before publication, Fitzgerald cabled Maxwell Perkins: CRAZY ABOUT TITLE UNDER THE RED WHITE AND BLUE STOP WHART WOULD DELAY BE. By then it was too late. And it is too late now to re-title a classic novel.

6.13 last autumn

Since Nick left New York after Gatsby's murder in the autumn of 1922, he is narrating the story sometime between then and the autumn of 1923. However, at 171.1 Nick states, "After two years I remember the rest of that day"—the day of the murder. The discrepancy may have been the result of Fitzgerald confusing Nick's chronology with his own: Fitzgerald finished the novel in the fall of 1924. The likeliest explanation is that Fitzgerald con-

fused years with seasons: two autumns but roughly twelve
months. However, it is possible that the extra year was deliberately built into the scheme of the novel to indicate that Nick has
spent the year 1923–4 writing the book—in order to strengthen
the impression that the narrator is the author.

6.16 Gatsby

The pun on *gat*, the slang term for pistol, is obvious.

8.12/10.6 West Egg/East Egg

The fictionalized geography of *The Great Gatsby* was based on
the actual geography of Long Island and the borough of Queens.
See map on page 206.

15.30 "You must know Gatsby."

It is puzzling that Jordan has not already told Daisy about Gatsby.
Her explanation at 80.8–9 that "even after I'd met him on Long
Island I didn't realize it was the same man" is weak.

17.18–19 'The Rise of the Coloured Empires' . . . Goddard

The allusion is to *The Rising Tide of Color,* by Lothrop Stoddard
(New York: Scribners, 1920), but it seems clear that Fitzgerald did
not want to provide the correct title and author. Lothrop Stoddard is not to be confused with John L. Stoddard, author of
Stoddard's Lectures. See Explanatory Note on 50.10–11.

23.3 *Jordan Baker*

This name combines two automobile makes: the sporty Jordan
and the conservative Baker electric. Fitzgerald informed Maxwell
Perkins that Jordan Baker was based on Edith Cummings, who
won the 1923 women's golf championship.

27.4 valley of ashes

Based on the Corona dump in the borough of Queens, a swamp
that was being filled with ashes, garbage, and manure.

27.17 retinas

The retina is at the back of the eye and cannot be seen. Fitzgerald meant *irises* or *pupils*.

33.18 "Simon Called Peter"

This popular novel (London: Constable, 1921) by Robert Keable (1887–1927) was regarded as immoral by Fitzgerald. The novel's protagonist is an army chaplain who becomes involved in passionate episodes.

45.10 Frisco

Joe Frisco (1890?–1958), stuttering comedian and eccentric dancer who was credited with inventing the dance called the "black bottom."

45.13 Gilda Gray's

(1901?–1959), star of the *Ziegfeld Follies* who introduced the dance called the "shimmy."

50.10–11 "Stoddard Lectures."

Beginning in 1897 John L. Stoddard (1850–1931) published fifteen volumes of illustrated travel books under the general title of *John L. Stoddard's Lectures*.

50.13 Belasco

David Belasco (1854–1931), Broadway producer known for the realism of his sets.

51.30–31, 52.1 Third . . . Ninth Machine-Gun Battalion . . . Seventh Infantry

The Ninth Machine-Gun Battalion (Sixth Infantry Brigade) and the Seventh Infantry Regiment (Fifth Infantry Brigade) were both in the Third Division. On 6 June 1918 the Ninth Machine-Gun Battalion (Nick) was at Château-Thierry, and the Seventh Infantry (Gatsby) was brought up to defend the town.

52.5; 57.30; 68.7 hydroplane

In the Twenties this word was applied to both motorboats and seaplanes. Gatsby owns a seaplane, for he speaks of "going up in the hydroplane" (57.29–30), and Nick says that he has "mounted in his hydroplane" (68.7).

52.7 old sport

This defining expression was probably taken from Fitzgerald's Great Neck acquaintance Max Gerlach, an alleged bootlegger. The connection between Gerlach and Gatsby is established by a note in Fitzgerald's scrapbooks: "Enroute from the coast—Here for a few days on business—How are you and the family old Sport? Gerlach." Almost nothing is known about Gerlach, who shot himself in 1939, when he was in the used-car business in Flushing.

70.22–3 two machine-gun detachments

Fitzgerald's revision reduces Gatsby's command to a size appropriate for a first lieutenant or captain and thereby reinforces Gatsby's heroism.

Although the Third Division was engaged in the Meuse-Argonne Offensive, this division was not in the Argonne Forest battle—which was fought by the Twenty-eighth and Seventy-seventh Divisions. The Argonne battle began on 26 September 1918. Since Gatsby states that he was in the Seventh Infantry Regiment "until June nineteen-eighteen," it may be assumed that he was transferred to the Twenty-eighth Division or the Seventy-seventh Division in time for the Argonne Forest battle. See Explanatory Note on 51.30–31, 52.1.

72.16 Port Roosevelt

This place has not been located either in Queens or on Long Island. The Northern Boulevard route from Great Neck to Manhattan passed close to the Flushing Bay Barge Canal Terminal, where Nick could have seen barges, which he describes as "red-belted ocean-going ships."

72.24; 132.3 Astoria

The Queensboro Bridge connects Manhattan with Long Island City—not Astoria—in Queens. Fitzgerald's friend the writer Ring Lardner reported this error to him after the book was printed, and Fitzgerald responded to Maxwell Perkins: "if you made the changes all right—if not let them go."

73.29 Wolfshiem

Meyer Wolfshiem was based on Arnold Rothstein (1882–1928), a gambler and racketeer. Known as "The Brain" and "The Bank-roll," he was credited with many criminal activities, from fixing sporting events to dealing in stolen bonds; but he was never found guilty of any crime. He was the victim of an unsolved murder in 1928. Fitzgerald noted in a 1937 letter to Corey Ford: "always starting from the *small* focal point that impressed me—my own meeting with Arnold Rothstein for instance." Nothing is known about the occasion of this meeting. See Leo Katcher, *The Big Bankroll* (New York: Harper, 1959).

74.26 Metropole

A Manhattan hotel near the corner of Broadway and Forty-third Street where Herman Rosenthal was murdered in 1912. He was alone at a table when called outside by a waiter; therefore Wolf-shiem's statement "It was six of us at the table" does not accord with the facts. See Andy Logan, *Against the Evidence: The Becker-Rosenthal Affair* (New York: McCall, 1970).

75.16 "Five with Becker."

Police lieutenant Charles Becker was electrocuted in 1915 for the Rosenthal murder, along with Lefty Louie, Dago Frank, Gyp the Blood, and Whitey Lewis.

78.3–4 fixed the World's Series

In 1919 the Chicago White Sox were heavily favored to defeat the Cincinnati Reds. Gamblers bribed White Sox players to throw the

World's Series, an event that caused national consternation when it was exposed.

Although Arnold Rothstein—the model for Meyer Wolfshiem—was suspected of having arranged the fix, it was never established that he was actually responsible. Nevertheless Rothstein did know about it and bet accordingly. See Eliot Asinof, *Eight Men Out* (New York: Holt, Rinehart & Winston, 1963).

90.24 Castle Rackrent

An allusion to the novel by Maria Edgeworth (1767–1849) published in 1801.

93.20 Kant at his church steeple

The German philosopher Immanuel Kant (1724–1804) was said to have been in the habit of looking at a steeple when he was thinking.

95.22 drug business

Gatsby owned drugstores; he did not deal in hard drugs. Between 1919 and 1933 the Eighteenth Amendment prohibited sale of alcoholic beverages. However, drugstores were permitted to sell whiskey by prescription, and some of them were fronts for bootlegging.

103.16 "underground pipe-line to Canada"

One of the myths of Prohibition was that alcohol was being piped into the United States from Canada.

104.10 informed Cody that a wind might catch him

The meeting between Gatsby and Cody was based on the boyhood experience of Fitzgerald's Great Neck friend Robert Kerr. Fitzgerald wrote to Kerr from France in 1924: "The part of what you told me which I am including in my novel is the ship, yatch I mean, + the mysterious yatchsman whose mistress was Nellie Bly. I have my hero occupy the same position you did + obtain it in the same way." See Joseph Corso, "One Not-Forgotten

Summer Night: Sources for Fictional Symbols of American Character in *The Great Gatsby*," *Fitzgerald/Hemingway Annual 1976*, pp. 8–33.

106.15 Barbary Coast

The Barbary Coast is the area of North Africa from Egypt to the Atlantic; but it is uncertain whether Cody's yacht was capable of transatlantic voyages. During the nineteenth century the San Francisco honky-tonk district was called the Barbary Coast; it is possible that Fitzgerald was referring to this destination.

119.3 Trimalchio

See Explanatory Note on title.

134.22 Biloxi, Tennessee

Biloxi is in the state of Mississippi; there is no Biloxi in Tennessee. It is impossible to determine whether this geographical confusion was the characters' or the author's.

169.25–9 heard the shots . . . my rushing anxiously. . . . But they knew then, I firmly believe.

The servants' awareness of Gatsby's murder and their failure to act are not explained. Perhaps, as "protégés" of Wolfshiem, they have been trained to ignore gunshots.

174.23 handed the bonds over the counter

An indication that Gatsby was involved in handling stolen securities, as Arnold Rothstein allegedly was. In December 1924 Fitzgerald reported to Perkins from Rome on the revision of his novel: "Anyhow after careful searching of the files (of a man's mind here) for the Fuller Magee case + after having had Zelda draw pictures until her fingers ache I know Gatsby better than I know my own child."

Stockbroker Edward M. Fuller and his partner William F.

McGee declared bankruptcy in 1922, with $6 million in debts. Fuller, a Great Neck resident, and McGee were indicted on twelve counts of fraud. During his four trials Fuller's close connections with Arnold Rothstein were made public. See Henry Dan Piper, "The Fuller-McGee Case," *Fitzgerald's "The Great Gatsby,"* ed. Piper (New York: Scribners, 1970), pp. 171–184.

176.24 James J. Hill

Railroad tycoon (1838–1916) who lived in St. Paul, Minnesota, Fitzgerald's hometown.

178.6–7 "The Swastika Holding Company"

Not an indication that Wolfshiem is a Nazi. Indeed, he is a Jew. Although Hitler took the swastika (an ancient Indian sign of good luck) as the symbol of the Nazi party as early as 1920, at the time Fitzgerald was writing the novel the swastika had no widespread exposure as the Nazis' symbol. It was simply a popular—and universal—decorative device, to be found in Roman catacombs, Incan textiles, American Indian artifacts, and Buddhist art, among other places.

181.12 "Hopalong Cassidy."

This cowboy character was created by Clarence E. Mulford in 1907, but *Hopalong Cassidy* was not published until 1910 (Chicago: McClurg). Therefore the 1906 date on Gatsby's copy is anachronistic.

Further Reading

♦

The Great Gatsby, ed. Bruccoli. Cambridge & New York: Cambridge University Press, 1991. Scholarly edition with editorial apparatus.

The Great Gatsby: A Facsimile of the Manuscript, ed. Bruccoli. Washington, D.C.: Bruccoli Clark/Microcard Books, 1973.

F. Scott Fitzgerald Manuscripts, 18 vols., ed. Bruccoli. New York & London: Garland, 1990–1; vol. III, *The Great Gatsby: The Revised and Rewritten Galleys.*

Andrew T. Crosland, *A Concordance to F. Scott Fitzgerald's The Great Gatsby.* Detroit: Bruccoli Clark/Gale, 1975. An alphabetical list of the words of the novel in context; essential for studying patterns of symbolism and imagery.

The Short Stories of F. Scott Fitzgerald, ed. Bruccoli. New York: Scribners, 1989. Forty-three stories—including the *Gatsby* cluster: "The Diamond as Big as the Ritz," "Winter Dreams," "The 'Sensible Thing,' " "Absolution," "Dice, Brass Knuckles & Guitar."

The Romantic Egoists: A Pictorial Autobiography from the Scrapbooks and Albums of F. Scott and Zelda Fitzgerald, ed. Scottie

Fitzgerald Smith, Joan P. Kerr, and Bruccoli. New York: Scribners, 1974.

Bruccoli, *F. Scott Fitzgerald: A Descriptive Bibliography*. Revised edition. Pittsburgh: University of Pittsburgh Press, 1987.

Bruccoli, *Some Sort of Epic Grandeur: The Life of F. Scott Fitzgerald*. Revised edition. New York: Carroll & Graf, 1992.

Publisher's Note About the Author

Francis Scott Key Fitzgerald was born in St. Paul, Minnesota in 1896 and was educated at St. Paul Academy, the Newman School, and Princeton University where he wrote extensively for undergraduate publications. In 1917 he left Princeton to join the army and shortly after his demobilization he sold his first short story to the *Smart Set,* edited by H. L. Mencken and George Jean Nathan. Fitzgerald's first novel, *This Side of Paradise* (1920), was published by Scribners when he was twenty-three. An exuberant and unconventional novel of undergraduate life at Princeton, it immediately established him as the bright light of his era—the spokesman for the "Jazz Age," a term he coined. That same year Scott married Zelda Sayre and the couple divided their time among New York, Paris, and the Riviera, becoming a part of the American expatriate circle that included Gertrude Stein, Ernest Hemingway, and John Dos Passos.

The crowning achievement of his career was his novel *The Great Gatsby* (1925), but Fitzgerald's popularity waned thereafter. In 1930 Zelda suffered a nervous breakdown that required her to be institutionalized. Beset by his wife's illness and his own drinking problems, Fitzgerald was having a difficult time writing *Tender Is the Night* (1934), for which he drew on both his own experiences and Zelda's fifteen months in a Swiss sanitarium. To accommodate the high lifestyle to which he was accustomed, he came to rely more and more on his commercial short story writing for *The Saturday Evening Post,* earning at his peak more than $36,000 a year. In 1937, he went to Hollywood where he worked on screenplays for the rest of his life.

Fitzgerald died of a heart attack in 1940 at the age of forty-four while working on his unfinished novel of Hollywood, *The Love of the Last Tycoon,* which Edmund Wilson considered his most mature work. For his keen social insight, compelling emotion, and breathtaking lyricism, Fitzgerald stands as one of the most important American writers of the twentieth century. His other works include *Flappers and Philosophers* (1920); *The Beautiful and Damned* (1922); *Tales of the Jazz Age* (1922); a play, *The Vegetable* (1923); *All the Sad Young Men* (1926); *Taps at Reveille* (1935); and a posthumous selection of short stories, essays, and autobiographical reflections, *Afternoon of an Author.*

A BRIEF LIFE OF
F. SCOTT FITZGERALD

The compensation of a very early success is a conviction that life is a romantic matter.

—F. Scott Fitzgerald

The dominant influences on F. Scott Fitzgerald were aspiration, literature, Princeton, Zelda Sayre Fitzgerald, and alcohol.

Francis Scott Key Fitzgerald was born in St. Paul, Minnesota, on September 24, 1896, the namesake and second cousin three times removed of the author of the National Anthem. Fitzgerald's given names indicate his parents' pride in his father's ancestry. His father, Edward, was from Maryland, with an allegiance to the old South and its values. Fitzgerald's mother, Mary (Mollie) McQuillan, was the daughter of an Irish immigrant who became wealthy as a wholesale grocer in St. Paul. Both were Catholics.

Edward Fitzgerald failed as a manufacturer of wicker furniture in St. Paul, and he became a salesman for Procter & Gamble in upstate New York. After he was dismissed in 1908, when his son was twelve, the family returned to St. Paul and lived comfortably on Mollie Fitzgerald's inheritance. Fitzgerald attended the St. Paul Academy; his first writing to appear in print was a detective story in the school newspaper when he was thirteen.

During 1911–13 he attended the Newman School, a Catholic prep school in New Jersey, where he met Father Sigourney Fay, who encouraged his ambitions for personal distinction and achievement. As a member of the Princeton Class of 1917, Fitzgerald neglected his studies for his literary apprenticeship. He wrote the scripts and lyrics for the Princeton Triangle Club musicals and was a contributor to the *Princeton Tiger* humor magazine and the *Nassau Literary Magazine*. His college friends included Edmund Wilson and John Peale Bishop. On academic probation and unlikely to graduate, Fitzgerald joined the army in 1917 and was commissioned a second lieutenant in the infantry. Convinced that he would die in the war, he rapidly wrote a novel, "The Romantic Egotist"; the letter of rejection from Charles Scribner's Sons praised the novel's originality and asked that it be resubmitted when revised.

In June 1918 Fitzgerald was assigned to Camp Sheridan, near Montgomery, Alabama. There he fell in love with a celebrated belle, eighteen-year-old Zelda Sayre, the youngest daughter of an Alabama Supreme Court judge. The romance intensified Fitzgerald's hopes for the success of his novel, but after revision it was rejected by Scribners a second time. The

A Brief Life of F. Scott Fitzgerald

war ended just before he was to be sent overseas; after his discharge in 1919 he went to New York City to seek his fortune in order to marry. Unwilling to wait while Fitzgerald succeeded in the advertisement business and unwilling to live on his small salary, Zelda broke their engagement.

In July 1919 Fitzgerald quit his job and returned to St. Paul to rewrite his novel as *This Side of Paradise;* it was accepted by editor Maxwell Perkins of Scribners in September. Set mainly at Princeton and described by its author as "a quest novel," *This Side of Paradise* traces the career aspirations and love disappointments of Amory Blaine.

In the fall-winter of 1919 Fitzgerald commenced his career as a writer of stories for the mass-circulation magazines. Working through agent Harold Ober, Fitzgerald interrupted work on his novels to write money-making popular fiction for the rest of his life. *The Saturday Evening Post* became Fitzgerald's best story market, and he was regarded as a "*Post* writer." His early commercial stories about young love introduced a fresh character: the independent, determined young American woman who appeared in "The Offshore Pirate" and "Bernice Bobs Her Hair." Fitzgerald's more ambitious stories, such as "May Day" and "The Diamond as Big as the Ritz," were published in *The Smart Set,* which had a small circulation.

The publication of *This Side of Paradise* on March 26, 1920, made the twenty-four-year-old Fitzgerald famous almost overnight, and a week later he married Zelda in New York. They embarked on an extravagant life as young celebrities. Fitzgerald endeavored to earn a solid literary reputation, but his playboy image impeded the proper assessment of his work.

After a riotous summer in Westport, Connecticut, the Fitzgeralds took an apartment in New York City; there he wrote his second novel, *The Beautiful and Damned,* a naturalistic chronicle of the dissipation of Anthony and Gloria Patch. When Zelda became pregnant they took their first trip to Europe in 1921 and then settled in St. Paul for the birth of their only child; Frances Scott (Scottie) Fitzgerald was born in October 1921.

Fitzgerald expected to become affluent from his play, *The Vegetable;* in the fall of 1922 they moved to Great Neck, Long Island, in order to be near Broadway. The political satire—subtitled "From President to Postman"—failed at its tryout in November 1923, and Fitzgerald wrote his way out of debt with short stories. The distractions of Great Neck and New York prevented Fitzgerald from making progress on his third novel. During this time his drinking increased. Fitzgerald was an alcoholic, but he wrote sober. Zelda regularly got "tight," but she was not an alcoholic. There were frequent domestic rows, usually triggered by drinking bouts.

Literary opinion-makers were reluctant to accord Fitzgerald full marks as a serious craftsman. His reputation as a drinker inspired the myth that he was an irresponsible writer; yet he was a painstaking reviser whose fiction went through layers of drafts. Fitzgerald's clear, lyrical, colorful, witty style evoked the emotions associated with time and place. When critics objected to Fitzgerald's concern with love and success, his response was: "But, my God! it was my material, and it was all I had to deal with." The chief theme of Fitzgerald's work is aspiration—the idealism he regarded as defining American character. Another major theme was mutability or loss. As a social historian Fitzgerald became identified with "The Jazz Age": "It was an age of miracles, it was an age of art, it was an age of excess, and it was an age of satire."

The Fitzgeralds went to France in the spring of 1924 seeking tranquillity for his work. He wrote *The Great Gatsby* during the summer and fall in Valescure near St. Raphael, but the marriage was damaged by Zelda's involvement with a French naval aviator. The extent of the affair—if it was in fact consummated—is not known. On the Riviera the Fitzgeralds formed a close friendship with Gerald and Sara Murphy.

The Fitzgeralds spent the winter of 1924–25 in Rome, where he revised *The Great Gatsby;* they were en route to Paris when the novel was published in April. *The Great Gatsby* marked a striking advance in Fitzgerald's technique, utilizing a complex structure and a controlled narrative point of view. Fitzgerald's achievement received critical praise, but sales of *Gatsby* were disappointing, though the stage and movie rights brought additional income.

In Paris Fitzgerald met Ernest Hemingway—then unknown outside the expatriate literary circle—with whom he formed a friendship based largely on his admiration for Hemingway's personality and genius. The Fitzgeralds remained in France until the end of 1926, alternating between Paris and the Riviera.

Fitzgerald made little progress on his fourth novel, a study of American expatriates in France provisionally titled "The Boy Who Killed His Mother," "Our Type," and "The World's Fair." During these years Zelda's unconventional behavior became increasingly eccentric.

The Fitzgeralds returned to America to escape the distractions of France. After a short, unsuccessful stint of screen writing in Hollywood, Fitzgerald rented "Ellerslie," a mansion near Wilmington, Delaware, in the spring of 1927. The family remained at "Ellerslie" for two years interrupted by a visit to Paris in the summer of 1928, but Fitzgerald was still unable to make significant progress on his novel. At this time Zelda commenced ballet training, intending to become a professional dancer. The Fitzgeralds returned to France in the spring of 1929, where Zelda's intense ballet work damaged her health and estranged them. In April 1930 she suffered her first breakdown. Zelda was treated at Prangins clinic in Switzerland until September 1931, while Fitzgerald lived in Swiss hotels. Work on the novel was again suspended as he wrote short stories to pay for psychiatric treatment.

Fitzgerald's peak story fee of $4,000 from *The Saturday Evening Post* may have had in 1929 the purchasing power of $40,000 in 1994 dollars.